ALL IN A DAY'S WORK

"What brings you here?" asked the Russian.

"Work," said Remo. "I'm an assassin. Right now, I'm working on the Treska."

"How do you know about Treska?" said the man.

"It's complicated, you know, government politics and everything. In any case, I'm here to kill you if you're Treska. You're Alpha Team, right?"

"We happen to be Alpha Team, yes, but aren't you overlooking this," said the man and jiggled the short British gun. By the time the man fired the Sten gun, his arm was broken. He did not feel the pain of the broken arm because one needs a spinal column to transmit pain impulses. The man had lost a piece of his about the same time the pain would have reached his brain.

The Alpha Team, sluggish with days of drinking, moved with surprising speed to their weapons. But by the time their eyes adjusted to Remo's movements, his hands were snapping through bone—quick silent kills. In seconds they were all dead. Had anyone been watching they would have thought: *"How could one man do so much?"* To Remo it was just another day's work . . .

The Destroyer

IN ENEMY HANDS #26

by Richard Sapir & Warren Murphy

PINNACLE BOOKS   NEW YORK CITY

DESTROYER #26: IN ENEMY HANDS

An original Pinnacle Books edition, published for the first time anywhere.

ISBN: 0-523-00992-5

First printing, January 1977

Cover illustration by Hector Garrido

Printed in the United States of America

PINNACLE BOOKS, INC.
275 Madison Avenue
New York, N.Y. 10016

For the great McAdow's of South Charleston, Ohio. Sam, Carol, Sam, Jr., Beth, John and Michael.

IN ENEMY HANDS

CHAPTER ONE

Walter Forbier surrendered his .25 caliber Beretta to the owner of a small bookstore on Boulevard Raspail in Paris, France, just as the first buds appeared under the fresh spring sun that early April day, and four hours before laughing men beat his rib cage into the muscles of his heart.

"You have no knives?" said the scrawny old man with a gray sweater and a two-day-old beard. His teeth were black from a gummy thing he chewed and rolled over his lips.

"No," said Forbier.

"No brass knuckles?"

"No," said Forbier.

1

"No explosives?"

"No," said Forbier.

"Any other weapons?"

"I know karate. Do you want me to cut off my hands?" Forbier asked.

"Please, please, we must get this over with," the man said. "Now sign this." He unsealed a plastic case and took out a three by five card. Forbier could see his own signature on the back. The man placed the white card on the counter, unlined side up.

"Why don't you have one with photograph and height and weight?"

"Please, please," said the man.

"They're more afraid of my killing someone than of my getting killed."

"You are expendable, Walter Forbier. Is that the correct pronunciation?" He had pronounced it Foe-bee-yay.

"That's the French way. It's four like in the number and beer like in the drink. Four-beer."

He watched his little pistol go under the counter. Forbier wanted to grab it and run. He felt as if he had lost his bathing suit while swimming, and that now, while thousands lined the shore, he would have to walk through all of them back to his clothes.

"That's all," said the man after Forbier signed the card. "Leave."

"What are you going to do with it?" asked Forbier, nodding to where the pistol had gone under the counter.

"You can get another when you're allowed."

"I've had that one for five years," said Forbier. "It's never failed me."

"Please, please," said the man. "I don't want you spending too much time here. There are others."

"I don't know why they didn't just call us home," Forbier said.

"Shhhh," said the man. "Get out of here."

Walter Forbier was twenty-nine years old and he was wise enough that spring morning not to expect to live to thirty. He had a knack for bad timing.

Five years before, just out of the Marines with a degree in mechanical engineering, he had discovered that almost everything he had learned before doing his military hitch was now useless.

"But I graduated summa cum laude," Forbier had said.

"Which means that you're one of the foremost experts in outdated systems," said the employment agency.

"Well, what am I going to do?"

"What have you been doing recently?"

"Wading in mud up to my neck, avoiding booby traps, and trying to stay alive in situations that did not lend themselves to longevity," Forbier said.

"Have you thought of politics?" said the employment agency.

Forbier had gotten married, just in time to find out that others were enjoying the same pleasures without the legal complications. On the honeymoon, his wife invited several pretty young things to their hotel dining table. He was amazed that she showed no fear of his being attracted to them. Then he discovered it was he who should be jealous. They were for her.

3

"Why didn't you tell me you were a lesbian?" he had asked.

"You were the first really nice man I ever met. I didn't want to hurt your feelings."

"But why did you marry me?"

"I thought we could work it out."

"How?"

"I didn't know."

Thus, without a wife and without a job and with a useless technical degree, Walter Forbier vowed he would not mistime his future again. He would get into something that was going to last. He looked around, and the one profession that looked healthiest was fighting the cold war. Even if America lost, there would be even better employment under the Communists.

And so Walter Forbier joined the Central Intelligence Agency, and, for $427.83 a month extra, a hazard mission called Sunflower.

"It's beautiful. You see the world. You travel singly or in groups. You get your extra pay and all you have to do is stay in shape."

"Sunflower won't be disbanded?" Forbier asked cautiously.

"Can't be," said the officer in charge.

"Why not?"

"Because it's not up to us to disband it."

"Who is it up to?" Forbier asked.

"The Russians."

It was the Russians, the officer had explained, who had started the whole thing. At the end of World War II, the Soviet Union had had an excess of highly trained killer teams in Eastern Europe. They were not mass combat troops, but specialists

4

in eliminating specific people. Most soldiers just fired away and advanced. These men could be given a name and could guarantee that the person, whoever he was or wherever he was, would be dead within a week. The Russian group was called Treska—which meant cod.

The officer didn't know why the Russians had named their unit Treska any more than he knew why the CIA had named its counter-unit Sunflower. The Treska had been crucial in the Russian takeover of Czechoslovakia, and even more crucial when the country had rebelled briefly. Their job was to make sure key leaders died just as the Russian tanks moved in.

"They're beautiful. Not one peep out of the Czechs. The tanks were only window dressing, sort of like a show of force. The Czechs lost because they had no leaders left living, nobody to tell the people to go to the hills."

"Why didn't we use Sunflower in Vietnam?" asked Walter Forbier.

"That's just it. We don't have to."

And the officer explained that the real purpose of Sunflower was to keep a counter-killer team floating in Western Europe, just so that the Russians knew that if they used Treska, America would use Sunflower. "Like an atomic arsenal neither side wants to use." America had it, so Russia wouldn't use it.

And it worked, he said. Except for an occasional body here and there, the two squads floated through Western Europe in relative luxury, each letting the other know it was around. But neither acted.

5

The only thing that could terminate Sunflower would be the KGB's decision to terminate Treska.

Forbier said he was looking forward to joining Sunflower, and he planned privately on being with the team in Rome in time for Christmas. He was off by 4½ years—and that was reduced training time, allowing him six months credit for his Marine experience.

Five years of training.

He learned French and Russian so well he could dream in them. He learned energy control, to be able to function for a week with only a half-hour's sleep. Parachuting for Sunflower was jumping out of the plane with your chute in your hands and putting it on in midair.

He learned the feel system of firearms. You didn't use sights, you used feel. Sights were mechanical, and fine to teach thousands of people how to get a bullet flying in the general direction of their target. But the feel system required working with a weapon so that the flight path of the bullet was an extension of your arm. You imagined a yard-long rod behind the barrel of the gun and the curving drop of your bullet, and, after four hundred rounds a day for four years, you just knew what was in your flight path. This had to be done with one weapon only, and the weapon became part of you. For Walter Forbier, it was his .25 caliber Beretta.

Forbier arrived for his first day's duty with Sunflower after five years of training, and got the instruction that he had to surrender his Beretta at a bookshop. He didn't even have time to exchange his American dollars for francs. His contact stuffed crisp hundred-franc notes into Forbier's pocket. The ride to the bookstore cost forty-two francs on the meter, roughly equivalent to ten American dollars. When Forbier entered the bookstore, he was a deadly instrument of foreign policy. When he left, without his gun and without even an explanation, he was a target waiting to be hit.

Once again, his timing had been awful.

But if he were going to die, at least he was going to have one good Parisian meal. Not a great one, but a good one. He somehow felt that if he headed himself toward a great meal, his luck would not allow it. But he might be able to sneak a good meal past his luck.

On Boulevard St. Germaine, he chose Le Vagabond, an adequate two-star restaurant. He began with Fruits de Mer—raw clams, raw shrimp, and raw oysters.

"Walter. Walter Forbier," said a man in an elegant Pierre Cardin suit. "I'm so glad I found you. You're really wasting a meal with Fruits de Mer. Please let me order."

The man deposited his black homburg on a chair next to Walter and sat down across from him. In perfect French, he ordered a different meal for Forbier. The man was in his early fifties, with an immaculate tan, the elegant smile of a Wall Street board room.

"Who are you? What's happening?" asked Walter.

"What's happening is Sunflower is surrendering its weapons. This is an order from the Security Council to the top of the CIA. The government is terrified of any more CIA incidents. They figure with no weapons, you can do no damage."

"I don't mean to be rude, sir," said Forbier, "but I don't know what you're talking about."

"That's right. The contact word. Let's see. This is the first day of spring. Subtract two letters from G, which gives us E and we have—Early End, Ethel's Earrings. All right?"

"Fine Friends," said Walter using the following letter of the alphabet half the number of times the previous letter had been used to him.

"I know who you are. No one uses the contact words any more. Everyone knows everyone else. Don't eat the bread."

"Am I glad to see you," Forbier said. "When can I make contact with the rest of the team?"

"Let's see. Cassidy is in London and retiring, Navroki is out, Rothafel, Meyers, John, Sawyer, Bensen, and Kanter were out yesterday and Wilson this morning. So that leaves seven more, but they're in Italy and they should be out by tonight and tomorrow."

"Out? Out where?"

"Out dead. I told you not to eat the bread here."

The man snatched the crust from Walter's hands.

"Who are you?"

"I'm sorry," said the man. "I'm so used to everyone in Sunflower knowing me. Didn't they tell you who I was in the States? I guess they don't bother any more with photographs. I'm Vassily."

"Who?"

"Vassily Vassilivich. Deputy commander of Treska. You would have gotten to know me better if

8

your government hadn't gone bananas. I'm sorry things worked out this way. Here comes the food."

Forbier noticed the man was armed. He had a trim shoulder holster tailored to the lines of the impeccable suit. Almost invisible, but armed he was. So were the two men looking at Forbier from the back of the restaurant. One was a giant. He was laughing.

Vassilivich said to ignore the laughter.

"He's a stupid brute. A sadist. The problem with long-term operations like these is that you live like a family with your group. That laughing man is Mikhailov. If it weren't for the Treska, he would be hospitalized as criminally insane. Like your Cassidy."

Forbier decided to change his order. He wanted a filet. When that came he complained the knife was too dull. The waiter, white apron swinging before him, disappeared into the kitchen to get a sharper one.

"Am I the last of the Sunflower?"

"In Northern Europe? Just about."

"I guess you're pretty happy with your success," said Forbier.

"What success?" said Vassilivich, swirling a piece of veal in wine sauce and carefully balancing it up to his mouth so the dripping sauce would not mar his shirt.

"Destroying Sunflower," Forbier said. He knew what he would do. He had been trained for five years to do something and if he were the last of the weaponless Sunflower team, they would at least go out with something on the scoreboard. He forced himself to avoid looking at Vassilivich's throat and

9

looked toward the kitchen on the left rear of Le Vagabond, from which the waiter would be returning with his sharper knife. He took a bite of the bread. Vassilivich had been right. The crust was a bit too cardboardy.

"When Sunflower is destroyed, we will have our way in Western Europe and England, and then, if we are not stopped, we will be sucked into America. And then, if we are not stopped, we will ultimately all find ourselves in a nice little nuclear war. So what have we won by destroying you? A battle in Europe? A battle in America? We had a nice balance of terror going here and your idiot Congress decided to live by kindergarten rules that never applied anywhere in the world. Your country is insane."

"Nobody's forcing you to work over Western Europe," said Forbier.

"Son, you don't know how vacuums works. They suck you in. Already there are people back home plotting brilliant moves for us. And it will all look so good. Until we kill ourselves. If you had lived, you would see. Just as we must take advantage of your being weaponless, so we will take advantage of Western Europe being weaponless, so to speak."

"Your English is very good," said Forbier.

"You shouldn't have eaten the bread," said Vassilivich.

When the sharper knife came, the laughing giant, not the waiter, delivered it, and, still laughing, cut Forbier's filet for him. Forbier declined dessert.

In an alley, off a side street near St. Germaine, behind a shoe store featuring high glossy boots, the laughing man and three others beat in the rib cage of Walter Forbier.

Vassilivich watched in gloom.

"Now it begins," he said in his native Russian, gloom on his face like the coming of a winter storm. "Now it begins."

"Victory," said the laughing giant, wiping his huge hands. "A great victory."

"We have won nothing," said Vassilivich. A sudden shower came upon the city that spring day, feeding the roots of the trees for the new buds and washing the blood of Walter Forbier from his young face.

In Washington, a messenger arrived from Langley, Virginia, with orders to interrupt a National Security Council meeting at which the President was presiding.

The messenger got a signature from the secretary of state to whom he was assigned to deliver the small sealed package. Under the first wrapping was a white envelope, chemically treated so that if anyone touched it, a black mark from his body oils appeared. The Secretary of State, wheezing from his paunchy weight, left a trail of black marks across the envelope as his pudgy fingers tore it open. The President looked on, occasionally sucking at the pain in his right forefinger. Someone had passed a document marked "Single, Lone" around the large polished oak table in the sealed room behind the Oval Office. It had been fastened with a paper clip. It went from the Secretary of State to the Director of the Central Intelligence Agency, the Secretaries of the Army, Air Force, and Navy, the Secretary of

Defense, and the director of the National Defense Agency. When it got to the President, he grabbed it in such a way that the clip plunged into his index finger, drawing blood.

"It's a good thing the Secret Service isn't in the room" the President said, laughing, "or they would have wrestled that paper clip to the ground."

Everyone laughed politely. It was no accident that the three water pitchers always ended up, bunched at the far end of the long table. Whoever sat next to the President somehow found himself nudging any close pitcher away. The Security Council had accidentally discovered that some classified documents were water soluble when someone had left a water pitcher near the President's elbow.

The Secretary of State read the document he had been handed, and in solemn tones, reflecting the guttural accents of his German youth, he said, "It was to be expected. We should have known."

He removed the single paper clip from the document and handed three loose sheets of gray paper to the President of the United States, who cut his thumb on their edges.

Everyone agreed that paper could be very sharp. The President asked for water for the cut. The Secretary of Defense filled one glass half full. He passed it up the table.

"Thank you," said the President, knocking the glass into the lap of the Director of the Central Intelligence Agency, whose turn it was to sit next to the President, but who complained that somehow the Secretary of the Army always missed his turn.

The Secretary of Defense poured another glass and hand-delivered it up to the head of the table where the President put his bleeding thumb into the glass.

"Be careful, sir," said the Secretary of State. "That document is water soluble also."

"What?" said the President, taking his thumb out of the glass and holding the papers in both hands. The right thumb went through the document like a spoon through fresh, warm oatmeal. The pages suddenly had a long thumb hole in them. "Oh," said the President of the United States.

"No matter," said the Secretary of State. "I remember what it said. Verbatim."

The Sunflower Team had been annihilated, said the Secretary of State. This team had been the counterforce to the Russian Treska which had operated so successfully in Eastern Europe. Sunflower had been destroyed when it was deweaponed. The weapons had been taken away for fear of another international incident. Now the Treska was loose, blooded, and there was nothing apparently to stop them.

"Perhaps a stern note to the Kremlin?" suggested the Secretary of Defense.

The Secretary of State shook his head. "They have their problems too. They cannot stop. We have created a vacuum they are being sucked into. They cannot not proceed. They have their hawks too. After almost thirty years of cat and mouse, they suddenly had the mouse in their mouths and they swallowed. What do we threaten them with in this note to the Kremlin? 'Be careful or you will be even more successful next time?' "

The Director of the Central Intelligence Agency

13

explained how the Sunflower worked and that it took a man—an exceptional man—at least five years of training to achieve the level of competence needed for that sort of clandestine killing. What was needed now to stop the Treska was another equally good small unit. Or a nuclear war.

"Or time," said the Secretary of State. "They will kill and kill until even the American public wakes up."

"And then?" asked the President.

"Then we pray that there is something left to fight them with," said the Secretary of State.

"America is not dead yet," said the president, and his voice was somehow calmer and his eyes just slightly clearer when he said this. In some manner, a decision had quietly been made, and he turned the agenda to another subject.

He canceled a meeting with a Congressional delegation that afternoon and went to his bedroom, a surprising move for a very fit President. He shut the large door behind him and personally drew the drapes. In a bureau drawer was a red telephone. He waited until 4:15 P.M. exactly, then picked up the receiver.

"I want to talk to you," he said.

"I've been expecting this phone call," came a lemony voice.

"When can you get to the White House?"

"Three hours."

"Then you're not in Washington?"

"No."

"Where are you?"

"You don't need to know."

14

"But you do exist, don't you? Your people can perform certain extraordinary things, can't they?"

"Yes."

"I never thought I would have to use you. I had hoped I wouldn't."

"So had we," came the voice.

The President put the red phone back in the bureau drawer. His predecessor had told him about the phone one teary day the week before he resigned. It had been in this very room. The former President had been drinking heavily. His left leg rested on a hassock to ease the pain of his phlebitis. He sat on a white doughnut pillow.

"They'll kill me," said the former President. "They'll kill me and no one will care. They'd celebrate in the streets if I were dead. Do you know that? These people would kill me and everyone else would celebrate."

"That's not so, sir. There are many people who still love you," said the then Vice President.

"Name fifty-one percent," said the former President and blew his nose wetly into a tissue.

"Ever the politician, sir."

"And what do I get for it? If John Kennedy did what I did, they'd think it was a little boy's game and some sort of joke. If Lyndon Johnson did it, no one would find out. If Eisenhower did it . . ."

"Ike wouldn't do it," interrupted the vice president.

"But if he did."

"He wouldn't."

"He wouldn't have had the brains to do it. Everything was handed to that man on a platter. World War II, everything. I had to fight for what I got. No one ever loved me for myself. Not even the wife. Not really."

"Sir, you called me for something?"

"In that bureau drawer is a red telephone. It will be yours when I am no longer President." The thought overwhelmed him and he sobbed.

"Sir."

"Just a minute," he said, regaining his composure. "All right. When that day happens, you will have that phone. Don't use it. They're bastards and disloyal and never think of anyone but themselves."

"Who, sir?"

"They're murderers. They get away with murder. They go around our country murdering civilians and you're going to be responsible for them when you're President. How do you like them apples?" The President served up a delicious grin amidst his banquet of tears.

"Who are *they*?"

As the former President explained it, John Kennedy—who never got blamed for anything—was really the one who had started it. Code name: CURE. "Basically, they were a vicious, disloyal pack of killers who couldn't be counted on in a crunch. When things were going well, they were your babies. But when the going got tough, so did they. They got going."

"You still haven't explained, sir. I will need an explanation."

The President explained. CURE had been organized because the government had come to fear that the Constitution could not survive the spread of crime. The government needed an extra boost

16

in that department. But the extra boost itself was a violation of the Constitution. So without getting caught or blamed, with nary a peep from the newspapers or from anyone else, that good old liberal John F. Kennedy had plucked a CIA man out of duty and set him up with a secret budget. It was a vast secret budget. It had a network throughout the country, and no one except the head of it—a New Englander who looked down on people from California because they weren't born rich—knew about it. It had an enforcement arm too—a homicidal maniac psychopath, and his teacher, who was a foreigner, and who wasn't white.

"Sir, I don't understand how no one would have heard of it by this time," the then Vice President said doubtfully.

"If only three know of it and only two understand it and if you can kill anyone you feel like, as free as the breeze without anyone complaining, you can get away with anything. But if you are the President of the United States and a Republican and come from California and if your wife wears a plain old Republican cloth coat, then you can't even get away with trying to save the presidency and the country. . . ."

"Sir. In my administration, I won't tolerate this organization."

"Then pick up the phone and say to them, you're disbanded. Go ahead . . . say that. Johnson told me about them and told me any time I wanted to get rid of them, all I had to do was say they should disband."

"And did you?"

"Yesterday."

"And what happened?"

"They said it was up to you because I was re-signing this week."

"And what did you say?"

"I said I wasn't resigning. I said I was going to fight. I said if those chicken livers won't support their President in his hours of need, I was going to put the screws to them. Announce what they were doing. Expose them. Get them put on trial for murder. I'd fix this CURE. I told them."

"And what happened?"

"What happens to all great men who don't kiss the ⸱'s of the liberal establishment, who stand up for America, who can be counted on to do the decent thing in a crisis."

"What happened to you, sir, is what I'm asking."

"I went to bed as I normally do, supposedly surrounded by loyal and competent guards. During the night I felt a slight tap and when I tried to open my eyes, I couldn't, and I drifted off into a very deep sleep. When I awoke, the world was way down beneath me. Way, way down. I was on top of the Washington Monument and the lights beneath had been turned out. And I was right on top of that needle, looking down. Right leg on one side, left leg on the other, and one man—I could only tell that he had thick wrists—was on one side of me, below me, and an Oriental with long fingernails was on the other. And there I was, in my night-gown, with the point of the needle sticking right up between the cheeks of my you-know-what. And the man with thick wrists said being a tattletale was naughty and that I would resign within the week."

"And what did you say?"

"I said, even if this a dream, I am your President."

"And what did he say?"

"He said they were going to leave me there and I begged him not to and he said it was either being left there, or them bringing me straight down to the bottom. With the needle in between. And in my dream, I said I would resign." He blew his nose fiercely into another tissue.

"So you had a bad dream."

The then-but-soon-to-be-former President shifted in his doughnut-shaped pillow.

"This morning, the surgeon general removed traces of limestone from the rectal tissue of your President. I resign tomorrow."

So it had been, and in the chaos of assuming the presidency of a nation torn by scandal, the former Vice President and now President had never touched that red telephone. Even now, after talking to the lemony-voiced man on the telephone, he did not know what he was unleashing. But the risk was worth it. There was a situation in the world that could lead to world war if it were not stopped. And the third world war, with all its nuclear horror, would be the last.

Quietly he shut the bureau drawer and said a prayer. Then he opened the drawer again briefly. Pinkies were always getting caught in that sort of drawer.

CHAPTER TWO

His name was Remo and he bathed his body in the blue deeps off Florida's west coast. He moved with the slow, crisp snap of a muscled fin through the green plants and rocks where crabbers plucked delicacies for the rest of the nation. There had been a shark warning that morning, and most of the pleasure divers had decided to spend that day with gin and lime and stories about heroism which rose with the ascent of the sun and the decline of the gin in the clear glass bottles set on checkered tablecloths, as the drinkers washed down fresh crab and baked mullet in sweet butter sauce.

Remo followed four divers with spear guns, fading in and out of their group, going ahead, falling behind, until the group stopped and pointed to him and made the signal for going up to the surface. The surface always looked so shiny from below. He accelerated up into it, like a porpoise, so that as he cut up into the thin air, the water dropped beneath him to his ankles, and at the apex of his thrust, it appeared as if he momentarily stood ankle deep in water. He came back down with a slapping splash of his arms that stopped his head from going under.

The divers broke the surface too.

Puffing and spitting water, they removed the mouthpieces that led to tanks of compressed air on their backs.

"Okay. We give up," said one. "Where's your air supply?"

"What?" said Remo.

"Your air supply."

"Same place as yours. In my lungs."

"But you've been under with us for twenty minutes."

"Yeah?" said Remo.

"So how do you breathe?"

"Oh, you don't. Not underwater," said Remo, and went back down, curving into the green-blue cool of the salt water. He watched the other divers come down in splashing, jerky, waving, energy-wasting motions, muscles that worked against themselves, breathing that had never been trained, minds so locked in what they perceived as the limits of the human body that even a thousand years of training would never get them to use a tenth of their strength.

21

It was all in the rhythm and the breathing. The brute force of a man was less than almost any other animal per ounce. But the mind was infinite compared to that of other animals, and only when that mind was harnessed could the rest of the body be harnessed. Year after year, human beings were put into the ground at the end of their lives with less than ten per cent of their brain ever having been used. What did they think it was for? Some vestigial organ like the appendix? Didn't they see? Didn't they know?

He had mentioned this once to a physician who had trouble finding his pulse.

"That's weird," said the doctor, meat and animal fat reeking from his body.

"It's true," Remo had said. "The human mind is virtually an obsolete organ."

"That's absurd," the doctor had said, putting a stethoscope to Remo's heart.

"No, no. Is it true or not that people use fewer than ten per cent of their brain cells?"

"True, but that's common knowledge."

"Why are only ten per cent of the brain cells used?"

"Eight per cent," said the doctor, blowing on the end of the stethoscope and warming it up with his hands.

"Why?"

"Because there are so many of them."

"There's a hell of a lot of filet mignon and gold in the world, but that's all used. Why isn't the brain used?" Remo asked.

"It's not supposed to be used in its entirety."

"But all ten fingers are and every blood vessel is

and both lips are and both eyes are. But not the brain?"

"Shhhh, I'm trying to get your heartbeat. You're either dead or I've got a broken stethoscope."

"How many beats do you want?"

"I had hoped for seventy-two a minute."

"You got it."

"Ah, there it is," said the doctor and looked at his watch and thirty seconds later said: "Hope and you shall get."

"Want to hear it doubled?" Remo asked. "Halved?" And when he left the doctor's office later, the physician was yelling that he got all the practical jokers and he had a lot of work and only a weirdo like Remo would play the kind of tricks he played. But it hadn't been a trick. As Chiun, his aged Korean trainer, had told him early on:

"People will only believe what they already know and can only see what they have seen before. Especially white people."

And Remo had answered that there were plenty of black and yellow people just as insensitive and probably even more so. And Chiun had said Remo was right about the blacks and about the Chinese and the Japanese and the Thais, and even about the South Koreans and most of the North Koreans, they now being unified under the decadence of Pyong Yang and various other big cities, but that if one went to Sinanju, a small village in North Korea, there were those who appreciated the true outer limits of the human mind and body.

"I've been there, Little Father," Remo had said. "And that means you and the other Masters of

Sinanju who have lived throughout the ages. And no one else."

"And you too, Remo," Chiun had said. "Transformed from pale nothingness and worthlessness into a disciple of Sinanju. Oh, never has such glory come to Sinanju as to be able to create something of worth from you. Wonderful me. I have made a student from a white man."

And overwhelmed by his own accomplishment, Chiun had gone into a three-day silence broken only by an occasional "from you," and then a swoon of awe at what he had done.

Now Remo moved ahead of the divers, flopping with their artificial fins, leaving streams of shiny air bubbles coming up behind them. Four bodies fighting themselves and the water. They used oxygen they did not need for jerkily pushing muscles they did not know how to use. They hunted the shark, and the shark knew with a kind of knowledge better than mere knowing how to move and do. For that which required knowing always had less force than that which was done by the body itself. So Chiun had taught Remo, and so Remo understood as he, like the shark, snapped and curved through ocean waters off the Florida coast.

He had never been a big man and now, after more than a decade of training, he was thinner yet, with only his very thick wrists to hint that he might be something other than a thin six-footer with a somewhat gaunt face, high cheekbones, and dark eyes, and a sensual quietness about him that could make an elderly nun kick over a statue of St. Francis of Assisi.

He saw the shark before the hunters.

It moved low and steady above clear white sand. Remo flashed the white of his body and gave short choppy flips with his hands to look like a fish in trouble. The shark, like a computer aboard a cruiser, zeroed in, and with great gray strength closed upon the man in a small black bathing suit.

The key, of course, was relaxing. The long, slow relax—and to attain this, you had to disengage your mind, for this was the shark's home, and a man was a lesser being in this ocean place. A long, slow relax—for to try to resist the rows of driving shark teeth meant the ripping of flesh and the loss of limb. You had to become like the rice paper of a kite, light and accepting, so that the shark's plunging snout drove into your belly and you collapsed around its great fins, causing it to snap its head in frustration at the light paper in front of its mouth, always in front of its mouth, never allowing it to get a mouthful of the beautiful white tender meat. And then you allowed the great force of its snapping body to bring your left arm under its belly, and there with sudden power the left hand closed, solid and eternal, on the rough, thick skin.

All this Remo did, until finally, as he and the shark snapped at each other, in one wrenching moment the shark's belly skin ripped out, and the shark swam away in its own dark blood, its intestines trailing behind it. And, tasting its own blood, in fury it attacked its trailing belly.

Remo went down in rhythmic, steady moves beneath the dark blood clouds above him. The shark-hunters puddled along, still unaware of what had happened.

Remo came up behind them and one by one snapped the artificial flippers from their feet, leaving bare white toes pushing around. The flippers lazy-dipped and pivoted their way to the bottom. Four pairs. Eight flippers. And to prevent them from retrieving their artificial flippers, Remo snapped off their mouthpieces and sent them to the bottom also.

The hunters fired off a few harmless spears. If they had dropped their tanks and separated one might have gotten back to shore. But they remained, futilely trying to retrieve their mouthpieces and flippers. The ocean currents carried the taste of blood, and two hundred yards off, Remo saw the first of the triangle fins close in on the helpless swimmers.

None of this could not be seen from the shore which was a good three miles away. Not even the divers' belts would be left.

Remo surface swam back to shore and emerged at a small cove near Suwannee in Dixie County. A small A-frame with a large television antenna overlooked the moss and rock incline. He heard high chattering squawks over the rise. Inside a large television screen had Lyndon Johnson's living face on it, the big catcher's mitt of a puss with the beanbag ears. No one was in the room. Remo sat down opposite the television.

Onto the screen came "As the Planet Revolves," an old segment. Remo recognized the age of the soap opera because people were still worrying about someone having an affair, as opposed to the newer ones which had people worrying if they didn't.

Remo heard the high rising tones of a familiar squeaky voice. It was Chiun. He was behind the house talking to someone.

Remo phoned a long distance number and heard a recorded message. On the beep signaling that he could speak, he said:

"Done."

"Be more specific," came the voice over the phone. One would think he was talking to a person if one didn't know it was a carefully-programmed computer.

"No," said Remo.

"Your information is inadequate. Be more specific," said the computer.

"The four assigned were done clean. All right?"

"That is the four assigned were done clean. Is that correct?"

"Yes," said Remo. "Are your transistors clogged?"

"Blue code, purple mother finds elephants green with turtles," said the computer.

"Up yours," said Remo and hung up. But as soon as the receiver clicked off, the telephone rang again. It was the computer.

"Use your blue code book."

"What blue code book?" Remo asked.

"Be more specific."

"I don't know what you're talking about with your garble," Remo said.

"Code book blue works off the date and the volume you were given four months, three days, and two minutes ago."

"What?" asked Remo.

"Two minutes and six seconds ago."

"What?"

"'Ten seconds ago."

"Oh. You mean the poem. Just a minute." Remo rummaged through a rusting cookie tin made vulnerable by the salty air. He found a sheet torn from a book. He did the counting of words from the date.

"You want me to blend a porcupine?" said Remo.

"Let me repeat, purple mother finds elephants green with turtles," the computer said.

"I got that. It means blend a porcupine . . . one, two, April six, divide by four. Add a P before the vowel. Right. Blend a porcupine. This is a great code."

"Breakdown," said the computer. "Hand up and hold."

Remo hung up and the phone rang as soon as the receiver touched the cradle.

"White House master bedroom. 11:15 P.M. tomorrow." The line went dead.

Remo quickly calculated. It was easier the second time. The message: "White House Master Bedroom, 11:15 P.M. tomorrow" coded itself into "Purple Mother finds elephants green with turtles."

Remo tore up the poem. Outside he found Chiun facing a grove of coconut trees. He was talking in Korean. He was talking to no one.

The morning air gently ruffled the delicate yellow kimono, the long fingernails moved with slow grace, the wisp of a beard caught every breath that touched a leaf. Chiun was reciting old lines from soap operas. In Korean.

28

"The set's on but you're not watching," Remo said.

"I have seen that performance," said Chiun, latest Master of Sinanju.

"Then why do you have it on?"

"Because I cannot tolerate the filth of the new shows."

"We're going to Washington. I think to see the President," Remo said.

"He has called us personally to remove his perfidious enemies. This I had always predicted, but no, you said the Master of Sinanju does not understand American ways. You said we do not work for an emperor, but the real emperor was in Washington. You said our emperor, Smith, was but the head of a small servant group. But I said no. Someday the real emperor will realize the gems that are but his to command and will say, 'Lo, we recognize you as assassins to the court of the great automaker. Lo, we have endured the mess and bungling of amateurs. Lo, we have shamed ourselves before ourselves and the world. Lo, we now unto this thing glorify ourselves with the glory of the House of Sinanju. Let it be done."

"Where'd you get that garbage?" said Remo. "The last President we met, we put on the top of the Washington Monument. This time, we've probably got to steal the red phone. If I know Smitty, there's a deposit on it and he wants it back."

"You will see. You do not understand the world, being white and younger than four score. But you will see."

Remo had never quite been able to explain to Chiun that Dr. Harold W. Smith, formerly CIA and

29

now head of CURE, was neither an emperor now nor planning to become one. For thousands of years, the little fishing village of Sinanju on the West Korea Bay had supported itself by furnishing assassins to the courts of the world. When hired by CURE to train Remo, Chiun could not understand first of all that Smith, was not an emperor, and second that, not being one, he did not want the current emperor removed by assassination.

Now Chiun felt vindicated, and his frail elderly parchmentlike face lit with joy. Now, said Chiun, people would not be shooting guns at other people in the street, but things would be properly done.

"Forget it, Little Father," said Remo. "No one's going to put you on television with a royal announcement. We'll probably be in and out of Washington—snap—that fast. Like the last time."

"Who was that man? He slept well protected."

"Never mind," said Remo.

"He had a bad knee."

"Phlebitis," said Remo.

"We call it coo coo in Sinanju," Chiun said.

"What does that mean?" Remo asked.

"It means a bad knee."

In Washington, Dr. Harold W. Smith was admitted at 10:15 P.M. through a side door of the White House and unobtrusively ushered to an office near the Oval Room. He was a sparse man, sparse of lip and smile or the amenities of the day. He wore a gray suit with a vest and carried a fine old leather briefcase. He had a lemony face and looked as if he had lived on white bread sandwiches of imitation spiced ham all his life. He was almost as tall as the President.

The President said good evening, and Harold W. Smith looked at him as if he had told an off-color joke at a funeral. Smith sat down. He was in his early sixties and appeared ten years younger, as though there weren't enough life in him to bother aging.

The President said he was deeply worried about the ethics of such an organization as CURE.

"What if I ordered you to disband tonight?" he asked.

"We would do it," Smith said.

"What if I told you that you may have the only existing organization that can save this country and possibly the world?"

"I would say that I have heard that before from previous Presidents. So I must answer from experience. I would say we can do some things to stop some things or to help some other things, but, Mr. President, I do not think we can save anything. We can give you an edge; that is all."

"How many persons has your organization killed?"

"Next question," Smith said.

"You won't tell me?"

"Correct."

"Why, may I ask."

"Because that sort of information, if leaked, could destroy our form of government."

"I am the President."

"And I represent the only agency in this country that doesn't have its dirty underwear spread out on the front pages of the *Washington Post*."

"Did you force my predecessor's resignation?"

"Yes."

"Why?"

"Must you ask? No one was running the government. You know that. He would have taken the country down with him. And you know that too. We still haven't recovered economically from that absentee President."

"Would you do the same to me?"

"Yes. If the circumstances were the same."

"And you would disband if I said so?"

"Yes."

"How do you keep your cover so well?"

"Only I know what we do. I and the one enforcement arm. His trainer does not know."

"You have thousands working for you?"

"Yes."

"How come they don't know?"

"In any given business, 85 per cent of the people do not know what they are doing or why. This is true. The overwhelming number of people do not understand why their jobs are done that way. And for the other fifteen per cent, you can generally keep them in isolated compartmentalized jobs so that one thinks he works for the Bureau of Agriculture and another for the FBI and so on."

"I can understand that," the President said. "But in your killings wouldn't the police be picking up fingerprints of your man, especially if there is only one doing all that ... what's the word for it ... work?"

"Yes, if the prints weren't already out of circulation. He's a dead man. His prints are on file nowhere."

The President thought a moment. It was dark outside in Washington, despite the lights illuminating all the monuments. He had assumed this office at a point when his country faced collapse and he dreamed only of the great hope America still held out. Tarnished hope, yes. But hope, nevertheless. It was not, he knew, an improvement in the living of man, just to declare your country the new wave and to have police arrest dissenters as in the Communist and Third World blocs. The goodness was in the doing. But to unleash this force he now had before him would in a way further tarnish that goodness that was America.

Still it was not an easy world. And until man found a way to live in peace, you were either armed or dead. He did not assume the world was at a different stage yet.

"I want to tell you about the Treska," the President said. He found Smith able to cut through details. No, Smith did not want extensive intelligence reports; anything that was formally given, he explained, created traceable links. Smith's team would be unleashed. You did not order them; you turned them loose and trusted their genius.

"I want to see them," the President said.

"I thought you would. At 11:15 they will be in your bedroom with the red phone."

"You've provided them some pass?"

"No," said Smith, and he explained about the House of Sinanju and how the masters really hadn't come up against anything new for centuries, because new protection devices were really just variations of old ones, and Sinanju knew them all.

The latest Master of Sinanju had been hired by

a former agent of CURE to train the enforcement arm. The first assignment of the enforcement arm had been to eliminate this agent, who was wounded and vulnerable. Unfortunately, too many assignments had been necessary just to keep CURE secret. Even the most recent one. Four men who worked for CURE and had found out a little too much and had bragged a little too loudly.

The President said he had not heard of any four men being murdered; he assumed the murders had been done separately.

"No, all at once," Smith said.

"You will not work in this country again. No domestic activities any more," said the President. "No more. I don't understand how four men can simultaneously disappear from the face of the earth in a country with a free press. I don't understand it."

Smith said simply that it was not for them to understand. They went up to the room with the red telephone, and at 11:15 P.M. the President said he guessed that Smith's men hadn't gotten through security.

And then they were standing in the room, an Oriental in a black kimono, and a thin white man with thick wrists.

"Hi, Smitty," said Remo. "Whaddya want?"

"My god. How did they do that? Out of thin air?" said the President.

"Mysteries innumerable," intoned Chiun. "All the secrets of the universe to glorify thy great reign, oh emperor."

"It's not a trick," Smith said. "No mystery. People don't see things that aren't moving and these two know how to be stiller than anyone else.

"Did you see them?"

"No."

"Could they do it again?"

"Probably not because you're looking now. It's the way the eyes work. Literally, we don't see most of the things in our field of vision." Smith started to add more, then realized he knew no more; he knew so little of how Remo and Chiun worked.

To Smith, the President whispered that the old Oriental looked too frail for a foreign assignment. Smith said that the President's least worry was the safety of the Oriental.

Chiun made a short speech to the President about Sinanju being willing to shed its blood for his glories, about how the President's enemies now lived on short rope, and how his friends had a shield and a sword. Moreover, the President had many enemies, close and devious, but this was true of all great emperors such as Russia's Ivan the Good and the gentle Herod and Attila the Benign as well as such westerners as the fair-voiced Nero of Rome, and, of course, the more modern ones—the Borgias of Italy.

The President said he was not happy about this and that he had wanted to see these two because this was a heavy burden on his heart, and that if his country had any other choice at this time, he would not unleash them.

"Can I say something?" Remo asked.

The President nodded. Chiun smiled, awaiting Remo's speech of loyalty to the emperor.

Remo said, "I started in this thing a long time ago and I really didn't want to, but I was framed for a murder I didn't commit. Well, I started learning Sinanju as a way to do my job, and in the process I learned what I could be and what others had been. And what I'm getting down to is I don't like the way you call the Master of Sinanju and me 'those two' or 'these two.' The House of Sinanju was here thousands of years before George Washington ever got his army strung out on a short supply line at Valley Forge."

"What are you getting to?" asked the President.

"What I'm getting to is I'm not all that impressed with whether you have a happy heart or a heavy one. I just don't give a bubbly fart about how you feel. And that's how I feel."

Smith assured the President that Remo was always reliable, awesomely so. Chiun apologized for Remo's insolence before an emperor and blamed it on his youth, he being less than eighty years old.

The President said he respected a man who spoke his mind.

"There's only one person in this room whose respect I want," Remo said. He pointed to the President and Smith. "And you two aren't him."

CHAPTER THREE

The first thing Colonel Vassily Vassilivich noticed, in the new glory days of the Treska, was a loss of discipline. Before, when the Sunflower team was always floating somewhere in the same European cities as the Treska, no man would go up in a single elevator alone, no men would get themselves stranded in the back room of a restaurant without someone on the street as a safety valve, and everyone kept in constant contact with the rest of the killer unit.

Now, as executive officer of the Treska, he would lose the whereabouts of men for days. They would run through their hit lists in half an hour, then go off to savor the delicacies of the Western capitals and only report back when their money ran out, smiling a stale whiskey smile, bearded, tired, content with their own dissolution.

When Ivan Mikhailov, the laughing giant, returned to a contact point in Rome, the Geno Restaurant down the narrow sloping street of the Atlas Hotel, he became enraged when Colonel Vassilivich accused him of returning only when he ran out of funds.

Ordinarily, someone like Ivan would have stayed on his farm in the Caucasus, taking over some of the chores of plow horses. But his enormous strength had been noticed early by the KGB, which brought such things as candy and radios and extra meat rations to the Mikhailov family, so that when young Ivan reached fifteen he happily went off to training camp at Semipalatinski, where top-graded instructors watched in amazement as he showed how he could snap two-by-four boards in his bare hands, how he could lift the back of an official black Zil limousine with one hand, and how he could kill. And how he loved it.

Semipalatinski was less than two hundred miles from the Chinese border, and when a People's Army Patrol got lost and ended up inside the Soviet Union, the school sent out an urgent message to the Fifteenth Red Rifle Division that the KGB unit would handle the Chinese patrol, while the Rifle Division sealed off their escape. The message really meant the KGB unit commander wanted to blood his trainees. The Rifle Division commander scoffed at the policemen and spies trying to do soldiers' work, but he had to accept the order.

Three brigades from the Rifle Division trapped the Chinese patrol in a small valley. The Chinese retreated up the sides of the valley to small caves, where they dug in. The Rifle commander wanted to shell the caves, roll in explosives, and go home if the Chinese did not surrender. KGB had other ideas.

When night fell, trainees of the KGB Treska unit were sent in with short knives, garottes, and pistols. The order was that for every bullet the trainees fired, they would receive a lash on the back.

Vassilivich, then an instructor of English and French at the school, waited that night with the commander of the Rifle Division. They heard an occasional shot from the caves. About 3:45 A.M., there was a scream from one person that did not let up until after 4 A.M. Then there was silence.

"We will have to shell the caves at dawn," said the Rifle commander. "A waste of Russian blood. That is what you policemen have done. You have wasted young Russian blood. You should stay to sticking a microphone in people's asses, is what you should stay to."

"What makes you so sure it's not the Chinese who were killed?"

"For one, those were Chinese weapons fired. For two, if your silly little boys had won, they would be coming out now. At first light, we do what we should have done before."

"They have orders not to use pistols and to stay where they are until light, so that your soldiers don't become panic-stricken and shoot at them, and thereby force us, general, to annihilate you.

39

Sorry, but that is the truth, general," said Vassilivich.

"Lunatics," said the general. But his staff officers were quiet because all military men were quiet when KGB was around.

Vassilivich had shrugged, and in the morning when the sun first broke over the valley, the Treska trainees came out singing and dancing. Ivan skipped out of the cave, juggling two heads in his massive hands, and each trainee had to empty his pistol to show he had killed without it.

The soldiers were left to clean up the bodies. Several of them passed out from what they saw. Laughing Ivan had to be told he could not keep the heads.

"Give them to the general of the guards, Ivan. That's a good boy. Good boy, Ivan," Vassilivich had said. And Ivan pushed the two heads into the general's reluctant hands and sniffled because they were his heads; he had taken them off the Chinamen, and why couldn't he keep them and take them home to his village when he had leave, because nobody in his village had ever seen a Chinaman's head?

"Your mother wouldn't like that, Ivan," Vassilivich had said.

"You don't know my mother," Ivan had whimpered.

"I know whereof I speak, Ivan. We can send her apples."

"She has apples."

"We can send her a bright shiny new radio."

"She has a radio."

"We can send her whatever she wants."

"She wants Chinaman heads."

"You don't know that, Ivan. You are lying."

"Not lying. She always wants Chinaman heads."

"That's not so, Ivan."

"She would if we gave them to her."

"No, Ivan. You can never keep heads again."

"Never?"

"Never."

"Once now and never again?" Ivan had asked.

"Never, Ivan. Not now, not ever. Never."

There had been other incidents, but Ivan had always responded to a firm hand before. When the American, Forbier, had been outed and Ivan had crushed his ribs with one hand blow and Vassilivich had said enough, Ivan had backed off, and Vassilivich had given him a friendly pat on the cheek and they had gone out to enjoy the rest of the beautiful spring day in Paris.

But now, in the dim Italian restaurant with the three plates of spaghetti topped with veal in cream sauce set before Ivan, Vassilivich found reasoning difficult.

"I not spend all money," Ivan said, and his two large hands brought out bowlfuls of ten-thousand-lire notes, equal to about twelve dollars American apiece. The Treska unit did not calculate finances in rubles but in the American unit of dollars.

Ivan plopped the money down on Vassilivich's side of the table. Vassilivich tried to organize them and counted as he did.

Ivan lifted one plate of dripping spaghetti like a small saucer and sucked it all down, veal and sauce as though it were the dregs of a tiny cup of tea.

He licked his lips. Then he finished off the other

two and asked that the basket of fruit on a counter in front of the kitchen be brought to him. The waiter smiled and with typical Italian elegance and grace presented the basket to Ivan. Ivan took the basket and began to swallow apples and pears whole, as if they were little pills. The waiter eagerly got the brown wicker basket back before the customer ate it like a cracker.

There were two sausages which Ivan chomped on like pretzels, and a half-gallon of Strega liquor. Ivan finished off his meal with two pies.

"There are 40 million lire here, Ivan. We gave you only 20 million. Where did you get the rest of the money, Ivan?"

"I not beat up people and steal," said Ivan.

"Ivan, how did you get the rest of the money?"

"I not spend all money like you say."

"Ivan, you had to get the money from somewhere," Vassilivich said.

"You give it."

"No, Ivan, I gave you 20 million lire three days ago. You lived three days on assignment and you came back with 40 million lire. That means you at least got 20 million lire from somewhere, assuming you didn't eat for three days, which I doubt."

"Count again."

"I counted, Ivan."

"I not spend all the money."

"Where did you get that new watch, Ivan?" asked Vassilivich, noticing a gold Rolex held by a belt to Ivan's immense wrist.

"I find it."

"Where did you find it, Ivan?"

"In a church. Priest beat up helpless nuns and

Ivan save nuns and workers and they gave him watch because priest so nasty to all of them, making them give all their things to the state."

"That's not so, Ivan."

"Is so," Ivan said. "Truth. You not there, you do not know. Priest a big man and very strong and very mean. He say Chairman Brezhnev stick his thing in sheep's asses and that Mao Tse-tung is good and Brezhnev bad."

"You're lying, Ivan. That's not right."

"You like Chinamen and hate Russians. You always hate. I know."

Gently, for that was the only way one dealt with Ivan, Vassilivich walked the lumbering powerhouse out of the restaurant and up the street to the Atlas Hotel and up a flight of stairs to a small room where he told Ivan that he must guard the room and not leave it. And yes, Ivan would get another medal for protecting the room, and yes, Vassilivich believed what Ivan had said. He liked Ivan. Everyone loved Ivan because now he was in charge of this very important room which he must not leave. There was drink in the refrigerator and Vassilivich would send up food.

He only realized he was nervous when, in the elevator going down, he found his hands trembling and stuffed them into the pockets of his trim Italian suit.

If he had believed in God, Colonel Vassily Vassilivich would have said a prayer. He walked down the narrow street again and turned into the motor underpass beneath the Quirinal Palace. His footsteps made hollow clicks in the tunnel. A small sporting goods store featuring ski goggles, guaranteed to be worn by Gustavo Thoeni, was still open. Vassilivich knocked five times. The door opened with a thin dark man nodding respect. Vassilivich went into the back room, windowless, with walls of unpainted cement.

Three men were at a table marking a clear, long paper. Vassilivich nodded two of them out of the room. One stayed. When they were alone, Vassilivich said, "Sir, we have trouble."

"Shhhh," said the man. He was chubby, like someone's little doll, but he was bald, and the flesh folded on his face like flaps on a poorly made valise. His eyes were small dark balls beneath salt-and-pepper brows that sprouted like timid wheat in the dry season. He wore an open-necked white shirt and a dark, expensive, striped suit that somehow looked cheap on his short, round frame.

He had the new light shoulder holster, just like Vassilivich's, except that his dangled without that flat invisibility that the holster was designed for. No matter. The man could not be underestimated. He had a mind that could solve three problems simultaneously, he spoke two foreign languages without accent, four languages fluently, and understood three more. He had what the KGB had always looked for in their commanders—force. It was a thing that could be felt by experienced men. Vassilivich knew that he himself did not have it.

The Second World War had shown some men to have it. A war was the easiest proving ground for it. Peace could allow subtle intrigue to promote men without that force to positions that required it. But General Denia, sixty-four fat, balding and graying, with sloppy clothes, had it in handfuls. He was the sort of leader that men who had known great pressure would choose, if the highest echelons had not already chosen.

Now he did not want to hear of troubles. He was opening champagne for his executive officer.

"Today, we celebrate. We celebrate what I never thought we would celebrate."

"General Denia," interrupted Vassilivich.

"Do not call me that," said Denia.

"This is a safe room. There is lead lining this room."

"I say to Vassily Vassilivich, do not call me general because I am no longer a general," he said, tears clouding his eyes and the cork popping open. "I am Field Marshal Gregory Denia, and you are General Vassily Vassilivich. Yes, General, General Vassilivich. Field Marshal Denia. Drink."

"I don't understand."

"Never before have there been such victories. Never have such a small number done such great things. Drink, General Vassilivich. You too will be a hero of the Soviet Union. Drink. Back at the central committee, they talk of nothing but us."

"We have a problem, Gregory."

"Now drink. Problems later."

"Gregory, it was you who told me that the surest way to death is undue optimism or undue pessimism. We have trouble with Ivan. There will be an international incident."

"There can be no international incidents. We are the power on this continent. From Vladivostok to Calais, there is nothing but KGB. Do you not understand what we are celebrating? Have you not counted the bodies? The CIA is all but inoperative

45

from Stockholm to Sicily. From Athens to Copenhagen, there is us and no one else."

"We are overextending ourselves, Gregory. America will do something."

"America will do nothing. They have castrated themselves before the world,. If you think we have gotten promotions, you should see what Propaganda is getting. It's obscene. There are enough ZILs and servants floating around the Propaganda unit now to make a czar jealous. To us! The future is now."

"Nevertheless, it is impossible not to encounter some reaction from somewhere, and we will be overextended. We can no longer control Ivan, and he's not the only one. We have men setting themselves up in villas. I have not heard from three whole teams for a week."

"I give you one order and one order only, general. Attack. You have never before experienced the collapse of an enemy. I tell you, we cannot make a mistake. It is impossible."

"And I tell you, comrade field marshal, for every action there is a reaction."

"Only when there is something left to react," Denia said. "Attack." He gave the shaken Vassilivich a sloppy hand-scrawled list with running champagne diluting the ink in two of the names.

Vassilivich had never seen a list like this before. There were twenty-seven names. When the Sunflower was about, there would be one carefully examined and chosen name with cross descriptions, so that precisely the person designated, and no one else, would be hit. There would be practically a book on that one person. Now there was only a list with names and city addresses.

In a list drawn as sloppily as this one, at least five of the names had to be incorrect.

"This is not an adequate targeting if I may say so," said Vassilivich. He refused the glass of champagne.

"I know that," said Field Marshal Denia. "It doesn't matter. Bodies. We give the central commitee bodies. All they want. And you will inform Ivan that he is a major."

"Ivan is a homicidal imbecile."

"And we are homicidal geniuses," said Marshal Denia. He drank the champagne so rapidly that it spilled over his chest.

It did not take Vassilivich long to analyze the list. It included everyone in the vicinity of Italy whom the committee thought might better serve their interests by being dead, including a good half-dozen persons Vassilivich judged had probably done nothing worse than offend some KGB officer somewhere along the line. It was a garbage list. Success was doing what the American Sunflower teams had been unable to accomplish. It was destroying the skill and cunning of the Treska unit.

When Ivan Mikhailov heard he had been promoted to major he wept. He fell to his knees, his weight cracking the ceramic tile of the floors. He prayed. He thanked God, St. Lubdinasivich, and Lenin, Marx, and Stalin.

Vassilivich told him to be quiet, his voice carried. But Ivan would hear none of it. He asked God to look after Stalin and Lenin who must be in heaven now.

"We don't believe in heaven, major," said Vassilivich acidly.

"But where do you go if you are a good Communist?" asked Major Ivan Mikhailov.

"Insane," said General Vassilivich, who believed that Communism would ultimately be the best form of government for man if a few kinks could be worked out, but wondered if the kinks might not be endemic to man. This line of thought led inevitably to the conclusion that man himself might not be ready for self-government.

"Insane, major," said Vassilivich. In the room was a refrigerator stocked with small bottles of imported whiskey and fruit drinks in cans. The hotel stewards checked the refrigerators every morning and put on the bill anything that had been consumed.

Vassilivich opened a 1½-ounce bottle of Johnny Walker Red and made notes on the list. The names were not even coded. Just a list. They might as well have handed him random pages from a telephone directory. There were no teams at his disposal to isolate and to set up the targets. With Ivan in this state of excitement at his promotion, he might just tear down a building to get to an assignment.

Well, even if the rest of the team was going to pieces, Vassily Vassilivich was not about to betray his training. He noticed seven of the names were Italian Communists, men he personally admired.

He and Ivan would make early morning hits of two each day, waiting to hear if their descriptions were put out over the radio, and then continue until their descriptions were known, at which point they would pull out. Already, there had been descriptions issued on Team Alpha and Team Delta. In saner times they would have been withdrawn to Moscow.

He was interrupted by Ivan's crying.

"What's the matter, Ivan?"

"I am major and no one is around to order around."

"There will be plenty of people to order around back home," said Vassilivich.

"Can I order you?"

"No, Ivan."

"Once?"

"Tomorrow, Ivan."

Just outside of Rome, in the small city of Palestrina, Dr. Giuseppe Roscalli made himself morning coffee and a light breakfast cake. He sang as he took the cake out of the old iron stove with the same bunched-up cloth he used to dry the dishes. He had been one of the pillars of the Moscowites, a small faction within the Italian Communist Party which favored following the Moscow line. At least until the week before, when a former friend of his had published revelations about life in Russia, and a day later had been crushed to death in an elevator. Dr. Roscalli was sure it was murder, and he was sure the Russians were behind it. He had wildly informed the Russian consul of this and threatened exposure. He was going to denounce Moscow.

He worked the lines of his speech in his head, already hearing the applause. He would accuse Moscow of being no different from the czars, except that the czars were more incompetent and had a cross on their flags instead of a hammer and sickle.

"You who claim to be the will of the masses are the owners of the masses. You are the new slavers, the new royalty, living in splendor and opulence while your unfortunate serfs labor for pittance. You are an abomination before all thinking and progressive peoples."

He liked the word abomination. It was so fitting because what Russia had promised made its reality so much more vile. Abomination. Only an American movie actress with cotton for a brain could fail to see it. Human beings, more and more, were recognizing the Communist menace.

He heard a knock and the announcement of a package for him. He opened the door. A well-dressed man held a small box wrapped in shiny silver paper with a pink bow. The man smiled.

"Dr. Roscalli?"

"Yes, Yes." said Roscalli and a giant of a man suddenly appeared behind the gift bearer. A massive hand closed on the mouth of Dr. Roscalli. From ear to ear it covered his face. He felt a thumb like a spike press into his spine, and still seeing everything quite clearly over a finger the size of a banana, he felt the lower part of his body float off somewhere, and then, as if he were caught between Spanish castanets, the life snapped out of him.

"Put the body near the chair, Ivan," said Vassilivich.

The package also came in handy that morning for Robert Buckwhite, an American on loan to the Italian oil industry. Buckwhite was a geologist. Buckwhite also worked for the CIA. In different times, he would be considered just one of their spies, to be watched by one of Russia's spies.

Buckwhite was a relatively minor functionary who would, on his death, be replaced by another relatively minor functionary. Nothing would be gained by his death, except another name for Treska to put on the body-count list it would send to the central committee.

So as Buckwhite returned to his home in the small town of Albano where his mistress waited, two men signaled his car to the side of the road. One had a package in a silver wrapping with a pink bow.

"Signor Buckwhite?"

Buckwhite nodded and his head did not finish the nod. His neck was shattered at the wheel.

"Take his wallet, Ivan."

"But you say we not steal."

"Right, but I wish to make it seem as if others steal."

"Can I keep wallet?"

"No. We throw it away later."

"Why take it if no keep it? Why? Why?"

"Because Stalin in heaven wants it that way," said Vassilivich.

"Oh," said Ivan.

Ivan wanted lunch. Vassilivich said lunch would have to be later because in towns where people had been crushed, big men might attract attention.

Ivan wanted to give his one order now, being a major.

Vassilivich said he could.

"I order you to have lunch now," said Ivan. "All

mens to have lunch. Immediately. Is order from Major Mikhailov."

"We will follow your order later, Ivan."

"Now," said Ivan.

He had two legs of lamb in garlic butter, eating them like lambchops, a gallon of Chianti and twenty-seven canolis, filled with rich, sticky white cream. A team of carabiniere bristling with sidearms arrived with the twenty-seventh canoli.

They demanded to see identification. They demanded that the two men eating lunch keep their hands on the table. They demanded immediate politeness.

Ivan burped. Then he broke them like breadsticks. One got off a shot. It went into Ivan's shoulder. It had as much effect as sticking a tack into a rhino's hip. There was another shot, but this too proved woefully inadequate. It was a .22 caliber short.

In the car, Ivan picked the small slug out of his shoulder the way teenagers popped pimples on their face by pressing the flesh together. He did not calculate that the Italian policemen had been using .25 caliber weapons. He did not reason that since the Italians were using .25 calibers, the .22 short must have come from somewhere else. He did not bother to think that maybe the only man who might try to kill with a .22 short would have been General Vassily Vassilivich.

Ivan held the little bloody nuisance of a slug up to the front of the windshield, then crushed the lead flat between two giant fingers.

Vassilivich felt his bladder release and his shoes become soggy. He suggested that because Ivan's meal had been interrupted, in Rome he himself would make Ivan a meal. In a dropoff flat overlooking Via Veneto, an expensive way station for fast flight and exit, Vassilivich ordered bags of spaghetti, boxes of mushrooms, gallons of wine and a side of beef.

He had to personally select the seasoning. He went outside to a small shop and got fourteen cans of an American rat poison.

At a small coffee shop, he phoned the sports store under the Quirinal Palace. There was no answer. He wanted to inform Denia that Ivan had become totally uncontrollable, and that he was going to make Ivan safe for the team.

Back at the apartment, Ivan was nibbling at the side of beef, taking handfuls. He watched Italian television. Ivan did not understand Italian. He was still working on Russian. He liked the pictures. It had taken him three years to recognize that English was not some fancy form of the Russian language.

Better than Italian television, he liked American cartoons. He had cried when a KGB officer translated Bambi for him. Shrewdly, the officer had told him the hunters were Americans and the deer communists. Ever since then, Ivan had wanted to kill Americans. His only trouble was that he could not tell them from Russians. Everyone looked alike to Ivan, except Chinese. He could tell Chinese from Europeans, and very often he could distinguish Africans, although when they were cleaning up the Sunflower team and taking out an American black, Ivan thought they were at war with Africa.

Vassilivich hacked off a twenty-eight-pound piece

of beef. He added five pounds of butter and three shopping bags of garlic. He baked it for five hours, then made a whipped rat poison sauce.

Ivan snacked it away by midnight. Lying on the couch, he closed his eyes. Vassilivich was overcome with relief. He discarded his small gun and holster in the closet, careful to wipe off fingerprints. He changed his clothes for the spares in the apartment. He burned his old recognizable garments in the bathtub and let the air out of the bathroom. He shaved off a small mustache.

He glanced at his watch. It had been an hour since Ivan had consumed the fourteen cans of rat poison. Just to make sure, he checked Ivan's pulse. When his hand touched the giant wrist, Ivan jumped up, blinking.

"Well," he said, "another day, another ruble." He laughed and complained of a mild headache.

Vassilivich took Ivan with him to the sports shop. No one answered the knock. The door was open. Ivan followed Vassilivich into the shop. Vassilivich whispered caution. He called out three different code signals in three different languages. When he used English, a voice answered.

"Hiya, sweetheart. Welcome to the first team."

A thin American ambled out from the back room. He had thick wrists. He wore a black turtleneck shirt and gray slacks and handmade Italian black loafers. He looked at Ivan, and instead of showing terror, he smiled. He also yawned.

"Who are you?" asked Vassilivich.

"The spirit of détente," said the American.

Vassilivich's shrewd eye saw no weapons in the

American's tight-fitting clothes. He heard Ivan behind him gurgle with excitement.

"Chinamens, Chinamens," said Ivan, pointing to
what had appeared like a golden cloth in the back
room. It was a delicate aged Oriental with a white
wisp of a beard.

Vassilivich knew that this time he could not
keep Ivan from keeping the head.

CHAPTER FOUR

Remo could tell by the weight, by the strong balance on oaken thighs, that the second man through the door brandished immense animal power. Iron-bending arms and tendon-thick neck. A skull armored like battleship plating.

Remo could also smell the meat heavy on his breath, and his body reeked of grape wine. Remo put a table between them. The man cracked it with a thundering fist. Remo danced back.

"Who called me Chinaman?" said Chiun. "What idiot called me Chinaman?" He shuffled into the showroom of the sports shop, his hands hidden like delicate buds in the folds of his kimono. The other man stepped back against a counter laden with running shoes.

The other man looked at Chiun as if observing a corpse. Chiun asked his name.

"Vassily Vassilivich," said the man.

"And the big idiot?"

"Ivan Mikhailov," said Vassilivich.

Ivan grabbed a long racing ski and swung it like a sword. Vassilivich was sure it would drive into the thin American like a spike. But the American, with strangely slow movements, somehow avoided the ski. Ivan lowered a fist down to the American's skull but the force of the fist only lurched Ivan forward and the American was behind him.

"Are you in charge?" asked Remo.

"Yes," said Vassilivich.

"Then we don't need Ivan," Remo said.

Vassilivich blinked. What was he talking about?

Chiun had a point to make. People in charge of things had special responsibility for people under them. And those sorts of people shouldn't let other people who were under them call other people Chinese, especially when they were so obviously and magnificently Korean. Chiun said this in Russian.

"What?" said Vassilivich.

"You are irresponsible to let that animal called Ivan run around loose."

How did this Oriental know? Vassilivich would have wondered about this if he were not witnessing a bloody horror before him.

As soon as the thin American had been told that Ivan was not in charge of them, he caught one of the big fists. With a floating flick of his fingers, he

57

briefly jammed a wrist. An elbow uncoiled from the American's waist and drove up with a hollow thud into the rib trunk of Ivan. Ivan came forward as though smothering the American beneath him, and the American's right hand was above the American's shoulder as if he were begging for mercy. The hand was under Ivan's chin. Ivan's mouth opened. There were two fingers sticking out of his throat. The American's fingers.

The American's foot went out so quickly, Vassilivich only saw it come back. Ivan's immense skull was caved, as if a knuckle had rammed risen dough.

Ivan landed on the polished floor, heaved once, and was still. The American wiped his hands clean on Ivan's shirt.

"Garbage," said Remo.

"My god, who are you?" gasped Vassilivich.

"That is not important," said Chiun. "He is nobody. What is important is the barbarism in the world today when innocent Koreans can be called Chinese."

"Are you Americans?" asked Vassilivich.

"No wonder it went around insulting people," Chiun said. "First I am called Chinese. And now American. Do I look white? Do I have a stupid pale expression about me? Are my eyes sickeningly round? Why would you call me white?"

"Look, Vassilivich," said Remo, "we can make this easy or we can make this hard. But no matter, we're going to make it. Now I know you're Treska or you wouldn't be here."

"I am part of a cultural exchange," said Vassilivich, using the first cover that came to mind.

"All right," said Remo, shrugging. "We go hard."

And Vassilivich felt hands grab his ribs and move him like a store mannequin to the back room. Chiun turned out the lights in the display area and locked the door. Vassilivich felt his ribs go blistering, as if touched by a hot iron. And so strong was the incredible pain that he did not notice there was no smell of burning flesh.

He was asked his rank, his position, and the names and locations of his men. With each lying answer came the pain, and it became so regular that his body seized control of his mind to stop the pain, and he was giving everything—code names of the teams, descriptions, zones, layoffs, contacts—and still the pain was there and he was whimpering on the floor of the back room where just the other night he had refused champagne. He saw the cork under a small couch where it had rolled and he wondered if Marshal Denia had made his escape.

He heard shuffling behind his ear.

"Now for the important question," said Chiun. "Why do you feel free to slander Koreans? What has prompted you to such blasphemy? What drives your crazed mind to utter such obscenities as am I an American? What?"

"I thought you were American of Korean descent," moaned Vassilivich. "I'm sorry, I'm sorry, I'm sorry, I'm sorry."

"Heartily sorry," corrected Chiun.

"Heartily sorry," corrected Vassilivich.

"For having offended thee."

"For having offended thee," said Vassilivich, and as the American lifted him and cradled him out of the room over Ivan's wrecked body, Vassilivich heard the Korean warn:

"Next time, no more Mister Nice Guy."

What had taken so many years to hone and refine, what had been drawn from an Empire that stretched from Berlin to the Bering Straights, what had fused the best of an indestructible people with an inexhaustible supply of facilities and money, now went in a week. And Vassilivich bore grieving witness to it all.

The auxiliary Treska unit in Rome itself, on Via Plebiscito, a half mile from the Coliseum, was first.

Remo remarked that Chiun had told him that his ancestors had worked in Rome once.

"When there was good work to be done," Chiun said.

"Ever fight in the Coliseum?"

"We are assassins, not entertainers," Chiun answered. "Strange people, the Romans. Anything they found, they would put into that arena. Anything. Animals. People. Anything. I guess they just liked rodeos."

Vassilivich shuddered, and then he felt the American's hands go up his spine and there was a great relief. Vassilivich realized he had been going into shock and by some manipulation of nerves in the spine, the American had prevented this.

He could hear the night revelry of the auxiliary group from the street. Giggles of women, glasses tinkling. Who said nothing succeeded like success? Nothing destroys like success was more like it, thought Vassilivich.

It surprised him that he did not even want to

warn his auxiliary team. He felt he should at least want to do this one thing. But he didn't care. All his training seemed to have dissolved in that back room of the sports shop. All caring seemed to dissolve. What did a general of twenty years' service in the KGB want now? He wanted a cool drink and nothing more.

The Korean stayed in the street with him as the American went up alone. A small police station near a closed and shuttered coffee shop was on their right. Behind them, a recent gargantuan marble obscenity built by a modern king. It had wide marble steps and highlighted some Italian on a marble horse. Floodlights showed the passersby that this was supposed to be important. The trouble with statues and monuments was that when you had them on every other block they became as common as trees in the forest, and if you didn't have a guide to tell you that this one or that one was important, you wouldn't even bother to look.

The laughter stopped upstairs. Just stopped as if someone had turned off a switch. The Korean seem as casual as if he were waiting for a bus.

"Sir," said Vassilivich, and then, on some survival instinct he was unaware he had, he added: "Gracious and noble sir. Gentle wise flower of our delight, oh, gracious sir, please bestow upon your unworthy servant thy awesome name."

The Korean named Chiun, with the wisp of a beard, nodded.

"I am Chiun, Master of Sinanju."

"Pray tell, oh magnificent one, do you work with the Americans? Are you part of what is called Sunflower?"

"I am part of nothing. I am Chiun."

"Then you are not working with Americans?"

"I receive tribute for my skills," said Chiun.

"And they are what, oh, gracious master? What skills?"

"My wisdom and beauty," said Chiun, so glad he was finally being asked by someone.

"Do you teach killing?" Vassilivich pressed on.

"I teach what has to be done and what people can do if they can learn. Not everyone can learn."

In a few minutes, Remo returned with a handful of passports. In that few minutes, the confused and brain-strained Vassily Vassilivich, general, had learned that the Oriental was a lover of beauty, a poet, a wise man, an innocent cast into the cruel world, and that he was not appreciated by his pupil. Chiun also was a few other things which he would not talk about.

Remo showed the passports to Vassilivich who gave the rank and real name for each one. He just had to look into the American's eyes once to decide not to try to throw out a cover story.

Remo gave the passports to Chiun, asking him to hold them. Chiun had many folds in his flowing kimono and could store an office there if he wanted to.

"I am now transformed into a porter for your garbage. Thus am I treated," said Chiun.

"Five passports. What's the big deal?" Remo asked.

"It is not the weight of the paper but the heavy and grievous disregard you show for a gentle poet."

Remo looked around. He hadn't seen anyone

else. Vassilivich was a KGB officer. Chiun, the Master of Sinanju, was the last of the line of the most deadly assassins the world had ever known. So where was the poet Chiun was talking about? Remo shrugged.

In Naples, they came upon the Alpha Team almost by accident. Vassilivich spotted one of the members and made a fast calculation. He felt better this noon than the night before, and with a light meal and a small nap in the car which Remo, the American, drove, his calculating mind was working again. The Alpha Team was useless anyway. He had lost contact with it days before, and only Marshal Denia's desire to keep the good reports flowing to Moscow had prevented him from administering discipline. So when he saw one of the members, the explosives man, he pointed him out. Remo parked the car and ambled up behind the man. It looked as if he were greeting an old friend with a hand clasp around the shoulder. Only if you noticed that the old friend didn't have his feet on the ground might you suspect that something could be wrong.

Had Vassilivich not had more than two decades in the Treska, with the constant training of the assassination teams, the sets, the picks, the rolling sets, so many variations of killing another person quickly and surely, he knew he would not have been able to appreciate the instrument called Remo.

This American was better than anything the Treska had ever seen or imagined.

The munitions expert was dead by the time his feet reached the ground, and the American was walking him across the street as if he were still alive.

"What skill!" said Vassilivich, his voice weakened by the admiration.

"Adequate," said Chiun.

"I didn't see his hands move," said Vassilivich.

"You are not supposed to," said Chiun. "Watch his feet."

"And then I'll see him move?"

"No," said Chiun. "Then you'll see nothing."

"Why is that?"

"Because I have devoted my life to training that ingrate, instead of spending it on a nice boy like you."

"Thank you, oh, gracious master."

"I live in America now, but I am sorely tried by its misdeeds," Chiun said, and Vassilivich's cunning mind grasped the opportunity. He commiserated with Chiun over Chiun's problems.

"Do not feel sorry for me," said Chiun. "The gentlest flowers are always those stamped on the most. The delicate is crushed before the gross and unseemly. This is life."

And Chiun told of the horrors of American television, what had been done to the beauteous dramas of "As the Planet Revolves" and "Search for Yesterday." Chiun, as poet, appreciated them. But now there was such a thing as "Mary Hartman, Mary Hartman," and they had people exposing themselves, and killings, and hospital scenes in which the doctors did not save people but injured them. Not what sort of dramatic doctor did more damage than good? Chiun asked that.

Vassilivich avered that no good drama should have a bad doctor.

"Correct," said Chiun. "If one wishes to see doctors mangle people, one should go to a hospital, not a television set. If I wanted to see stupid and careless and incompetent doctors, I have only to drop in on a local practitioner, and my chances are very good. Especially in your country, you should know that."

Vassilivich gulped but agreed. What, he wanted to know, did Chiun teach this ungrateful Remo?

"Decency," Chiun said. "Love, decency, and beauty."

Meanwhile, across town in a luxurious villa overlooking the Bay of Naples, blue in the midday sun of the Italian coast, Remo was putting his love, decency, and beauty to work.

He had gotten the number and the location of the other operatives from the explosives man in the street, whom he decently dumped afterwards into a big vat of garbage in an alley where no one would notice him until the body started to stink.

He made his way to the beautiful villa. It was noon and everyone appeared groggy from the night's revelry. One man, his belly already going to paunch, looked up from his morning vodka and orange juice. He pointed a short British sten gun at Remo while he nibbled on a grape.

"Buon giorno," he said sleepily.

"Good morning," said Remo.

"What brings you here?" asked the Russian. The others still did not go for their guns but continued on into their boozy morning. One unarmed man was not enough to cause excitement.

"Work," said Remo.

"What is your work?"

"I'm an assassin. Right now, I'm working on the Treska. Is that how you pronounce it? Treska?" Remo glanced outside at the glistening bay and felt the cool spring breeze come through the green trees and the open windows bright with sun. It was a good land. He smelled the salt water.

"How do you know about Treska?" said the man.

"Oh, yeah," said Remo as an afterthought. "It's complicated, you know, government politics and everything, but basically I'm replacing the Daisy or is it the Sunflower, I forget these stupid names. In any case, I'm here to kill you if you're Treska. You're Alpha Team, right?"

"We happen to be Alpha Team, yes, but aren't you overlooking this?" said the man and jiggled the short British gun.

"Nah," said Remo. "By the way, what does this rent for a month?"

"I don't know. It's in lire. You keep filling baskets to the top and when the landlord starts to smile you stop filling. Lire. A virtually worthless currency."

"Anybody outside from Alpha?"

"We're all here except Fyodor."

"Well-built guy, blondish, with a funny smile?" asked Remo.

"That's him. But he doesn't have a funny smile."

"He does now," Remo said. By the time the man fired the Sten gun, his arm was broken. He did not feel the pain of the broken arm because one needs

66

a spinal column to transmit pain impulses. The man had lost a piece of his about the same time the pain would have reached his brain.

The Alpha Team, sluggish with days of drinking, moved with surprising speed to their weapons. Training overcame the boozy blood of their systems and adrenalin ignited their bodies. But they fought as though they had a target who moved no faster than an athlete, an ordinary athlete who did not know the rhythms of his body, whose hands were the same as a skillful soldiers' hands.

By the time their eyes adjusted to Remo's movements, his hands were snapping through bone, making quick, silent kills. He worked the chests that noon in the villa off the Italian coast. It took him longer to collect the passports. Back at the car in Naples proper, he asked Vassilivich to write down the correct names and ranks on each of the passports Alpha Team had used as covers.

"They are all dead?" asked Vassilivich, believing because he had seen what this man had done to the gigantic Ivan, but still horrified at the thought that one man could do so much.

"Sure," said Remo, as if someone had asked if he had put a candy wrapper in a trash can.

Beta Team was on a full alert, as it had been trained to be if contact was severed. The team had a small house in Farfa, a town overlooking the murky Tiber River, an Italian sewer since the days of the Etruscan kings.

"They really let the place go to rot," Chiun confided. "The history of Sinanju tells of lovely temples of Apollo and Venus near here."

"The House of Sinanju is an old institution then?" asked Vassilivich.

"Modestly so," said Chiun. "Aged with reason and tempered with love."

Remo at the wheel turned around sharply. He would have sworn that Chiun had been talking about Sinanju.

The American, Vassilivich realized, had spotted the first Beta outpost before he had. And he knew what to look for.

When the American left the car, Vassilivich asked how Remo had known that the man who appeared to be casually sunning himself on a small cement bench was really a lookout?

"That's where the outlook should be," said Chiun. "But these are matters of work. Would you like to hear a poem I have written?"

Vassilivich said, "By all means." He watched the American sit down next to the lookout who appeared to be sunning himself. The American spoke a few words.

Vassilivich looked on with dread fascination. The lookout was knife-skilled at the highest levels. He saw his man slip a blade from a sleeve on the far side, hidden from the American. Good, he thought. We have a chance. Good for you, soldier of the Treska, sword and shield of the party. The Korean, Chiun, was squeaking away in a language Vassilivich did not recognize. Chiun brought his attention to the back seat of the car with a gentle touch of a long fingernail to his throat.

"Perhaps you do not recognize classic Ung poetry?"

"Sir?" said Vassilivich. He saw his man smile politely. The knife was going to come soon. They were going to get back on the scoreboard against this killer team.

"In Ung poetry, the classic form is to omit every third consonant and every second vowel. That is the English translation of the formula. You know English."

"Yes," said Vassilivich. Any moment now the knife would fly into the American's throat.

"Then you would understand that the great Ung poetry disappeared about 800 B.C. I am not talking about common Ung poetry used until the seventh century. What so fascinates you out there?"

"I was just watching the American."

"Doing what?"

"Talking to that man."

"He is not talking," said Chiun. "He is going to do work. It is mundane. Now there is an especially beautiful passage I am working on ... what so fascinates you?"

The knife flashed in the bright Italian sun and the man smiled foolishly as if he had swallowed a balloon and should have known better. Vassilivich could not see the man's knife. The American appeared to be shaking that hand as if saying goodbye. The lookout nodded off to sleep. With a lapful of blood.

"The greatness of this poem is that it bares the essence of the flower petal and the sounds themselves become the petal," said Chiun.

Vassilivich's body was moist with prickly sweat. He smiled as he heard the Korean's high-pitched voice go higher as though scratching a blackboard on the ceiling.

He remembered vaguely hearing of this arcane poetry. A British explorer had said it sounded like a hysterectomy performed with blunt spoons.

Ancient Persian emperors were especially fond of it. Vassilivich did not know it had survived past the third century A.D. In some way, this aged Oriental had a close relationship with this amazing American killer.

Vassilivich had to figure out what. Was the old Korean a poetry teacher? A friend? He certainly wasn't a servant, even though he complained he was being treated as one. *Sinanju*. He had heard that name before. The old man had said assassins came from there, but certainly this frail, parched being could not be a killer. Yet, there was a link here. And one that could be exploited. Must be exploited.

The squeaky up and down of the Ung ode ceased. Remo, the American, strolled back to the car with twelve passports.

Vassilivich saw the lives of the Beta Team dropped in his lap. This was not a drunken crew gone sloppy. This was a prime unit at peak. They had not even gotten to their guns; he had not heard shots.

He wrote down their true Russians names and ranks. He knew every one of them. Some farm boys, some city boys, one even released from Lubyanka prison in Moscow, a homicidal maniac whom Vassilivich had personally trained to control his killer urges and direct them toward the welfare of the state. He thought of the training of each one as he wrote in the names, crossing off their fake Rumanian and Bulgarian identities. Ten years training, eleven years, eight years, twelve years. When young boys showed extra abilities, extra cunning and strength, the Treska had its pick of them.

It was at the time when the members of the Beta Team were boys that the then Major Vassilivich had insisted that families should be consulted before their sons were brought into the Treska.

At the time this had been heresy, but Vassilivich had been proven correct. If the family was behind the boy, then he went with a lighter heart. If the family received extra rations and extra privileges, then each boy felt he was doing something especially worthy, and every leave home would be a reinforcement of his loyalty to the Treska, not a strain against it.

He had won that battle with General Denia of the old school, who had preferred that families be separated as much as possible.

"We need men, machines, not little boys," had said the then General Denia. "When we fought the White Armies, the Treska—it was called the Chekka then—dragged us from our homes and made us men immediately. You kill or die. That is what it was; that is what it is, and that is what it will always be. Always."

"Sir," Major Vassilivich had said. "We have a 20 per cent defection rate now. That's high. Perhaps the highest of any service."

"It is a hard business we are in. They do not make men like they used to."

"I beg to disagree, sir. You snatch a fifteen-year-old boy out of school and tell the parents that he has been selected for the Olympic teams, or something else that they know is not true, and they worry; he worries, and sooner or later he is either going to defect in the West or desert back here."

"And we hang the little bastard."

"May I pose a question, and I place my life on the answer. When things get a bit untidy in the West and we lose an occasional man to the American Sunflower, what happens?"

General Denia had shrugged, showing he did not know what his shrewd aide was driving at.

"At headquarters I make a little mark in our records," Vassilivich had said.

"Yes, so?" Denia had been impatient.

"Have you ever looked at the file drawer where those records are kept?"

"No. I am not much for paperwork," General Denia had answered.

"Both defections and those killed in action are in the same cabinets. Defections are eighteen times thicker than those who died at American hands. We do almost twenty times as much damage to ourselves as the capitalists do to us."

"Hmmmm," Denia had said suspiciously.

"What I am asking is that we, at least, make the capitalist bastards destroy us instead of doing it to ourselves."

"As you say, your life," Denia had agreed.

Within the first year, desertions dropped and defections became unknown. Vassilivich had created an atmosphere where the teams knew that no other government and no other place offered them such honor and wealth. What the rest of the system did by force and propaganda, the Treska accomplished better by services and rewards.

It became a joke at the Dzerzhinsky Square Building in Moscow that the next thing the Treska would do would be to declare stock dividends and give out colored television sets.

But the jokes stopped when a small Treska unit, isolated from the bufferings of flanking units, and outnumbered forty to one, fought to the last man in the hills of Greece, despite lavish offerings from the Sunflower units to defect.

Vassilivich, back at training headquarters, made a big ceremony honoring the fallen men. If there had been a cross at the altar instead of a picture of Lenin, one could have called the ceremony a mass.

It was also Vassilivich who created the light coexistence with Sunflower, an almost friendly relationship as the teams watched each other and circled each other across Western Europe. It was also Vassilivich who, on the very day American CIA headquarters ordered their Sunflower units to surrender their weapons, led the fast, vicious sweep of the continent.

As mangled American bodies were shipped home for closed-coffin burials, including the very unfortunate Walter Forbier, KGB had intercepted a strange message:

Could have been worse. We might have been caught doing dirty tricks.

It was a message to Washington from a high-ranking State Department official, and Vassilivich, reading it, had thought: "We may be matched against lunatics."

But Treska had not been. And it occurred to

Vassilivich, sitting in the back seat of the car with the Korean poet named Chiun, that perhaps this all had been a gigantic trap. What a brilliant trap. He had never figured Americans for that sort of cunning. To sacrifice an entire strata of units so that your enemy would relax in time for your first team to mop them up.

That was what the American had said in the sports shop. "Welcome to the first team." It was a ruthless maneuver, but brilliant.

Yet Vassilivich, ever the analyst, was still bothered. True. It was a brilliant and cunning move. But Americans never thought like that.

They had always been geniuses with gadgets and morons at maneuver. Vassilivich felt a tickle at his throat. The Korean informed him that the best part of the poem was yet to come.

CHAPTER FIVE

It was a grand reunion. It was a glorious occasion.
Vodka bottles stretched thirty meters along a linen
tablecloth, each bottle with a gloved servant behind it. Accordions played. Glasses cracked against
the inlaid wood walls. Shiny boots clicked on the
polished marble. Blue uniforms with red piping,
medaled as though jewelers had run amok, shone
on proud chests.

Someone yelled out in the thick eastern accent
of Vladivostok: "He's coming! He's coming!"

Silence came, marred only by the last few crashes
of glasses from officers who had not realized what
was happening. And then only the footsteps of a

single man. A man at a podium set high at the far end of the hall called out:

"Officers, members of the committee, sword and shield of the party, we now greet with admiration, a hero of the Soviet Socialist Republic, Field Marshal Gregory Denia. A bravo for Denia."

"Bravo, Bravo," yelled the crowd.

Denia, medaled across his fat chest, his round face gleaming joy, his pudgy hands raised above him in his own triumph, marched into the great hall of the people's Committee for State Security.

"Denia. Denia. Denia," came the chant.

And he waved furiously, smiling at old friends, survivors of the great war where two nations battled in a line from sea to sea, with the losers facing annihilation. They were tough men, these officers, survivors of the purges, the favorites of Stalin, then Beria, then Krushchev, and finally the current chairman. Chairmen came and went. The KGB stayed forever. Denia signaled for silence.

And then he spoke.

"I am not at liberty to tell all of you the specifics of our victory. I am not at liberty to tell you just how we achieved more than prominence in Western Europe. But I can tell you this, comrades. Today, the Union of Soviet Socialist Republics dominates her continent as no nation ever has. Europe is ours. Tomorrow Asia and then the world. Tomorrow the world. Tomorrow the world."

Many officers who had fought only the cold war against America, in grueling, stalking contests where victories were measured in mere inches, now screamed their praise. For with Field Marshal

Denia there had been a recent breakthrough of miles. The West was in full retreat.

Of course, even in such a work-oriented group, there was always the one wag. From the back of the room, someone yelled out a toast to Russia's greatest ally.

"Bravo for the United States Congress and its investigating committees."

Faces turned in scorn, but Field Marshal Denia smiled.

"Yes, we have had help. But it was not accidental. Did not Lenin himself say the capitalists would hang themselves if we gave them enough rope? Well, they have the rope, and we tied the knot."

Denia called for a full bottle of vodka, and then, resting on the polished heels of his leather boots, leaned back and downed it completely to a chorus of encouragement. Then he danced out into the center of the marble hall to great clapping. A captain, his face ashen, his hands trembling, worked his way toward the clearing where Denia now spun drunkenly, laughing. The captain, in dull green, made a striking contrast to the array of medals, like a cheap plastic bowl in a jewelry store display window.

Denia brushed aside the captain.

"Comrade marshal, it is of the utmost urgency," said the captain.

He handed Denia a double-sealed envelope, the kind where a small plastic shield has to be broken to open it. He also handed the marshal a pen which he wanted him to use to sign for the letter. Denia took the pen and flipped it into the air.

"I need your signature, marshal."

"Anatoli, tell this idiot he doesn't need a signature."

"You don't need Marshal Denia's signature, captain," came a voice from the crowd. It was the commander of the captain's entire unit.

Denia read the message. He was feeling good with the warmth of the vodka, and his blood was running hot and wild from dancing. The message read:

> Apparent high complications Treska units southern flank Europe. Stop. Suggest your immediate return Dzerzhinsky Square Building for consultation. Stop. Immediately.

Denia crumpled the note and put it back in his pocket.

"Serious, Gregory?" asked a general.

Denia shrugged. "It is always serious. The central committee wants to change the color of the uniforms and so the chairman of a textile factory faces a serious problem. The ministry of propaganda hears about a Solzhenitsyn speech or a new book he has written and they have a serious problem. Every day there is a new serious problem here and there, but all of us are drinking good vodka and living in good homes and yet everyone goes running around crying the sky is falling. The sky, gentlemen, is still above us as it was before we went crying from our mother's wombs into a serious confrontation with air, and it will be there after we are shoveled into ground following a serious confrontation with death. Comrades, I tell all of you now. There is no such thing as a serious thing."

His little speech was greeted with applause, partly because he held the rank of marshal, but also because he was known as a man who held things together during crunches. So this was the marshal's philosophy, and it was respected.

Outside a black Zil limousine was waiting. Traffic at home was always so much easier than in the field, where so many people had cars.

Marshal Denia was not as casual as he had appeared at his celebration. Years in the field had given him that extra sense of when to worry and when not to. It was a time for worrying.

Lubyanka Prison was in the Dzherzhinsky Square building. So many of his comrades had ended up there during Stalin's reign. He was the only one to survive from his unit, a political one under the command of a former university professor who had joined what was then called the Chekka, to be changed to the OGPU, to be changed to the NKVD, the MVD, and, finally the KGB. All different clothes for the same body.

Stalin had wanted the whole unit, forty-two men, to dress in formal attire and attend a dinner with him alone. There was much vodka. Something had told Denia not to indulge too much on that long-ago evening in the early thirties. Perhaps it was the absence of water on the long tables that had given him the clue that Stalin wanted them to drink heavily.

His commander, who ordinarily was a cautious, abstemious man given to tea and crackers, had downed vodka as if he had been born on the back of a Cossack horse. By mid-meal, the commander had been talking loudly of being part of the socialist vanguard. Stalin had smiled. He did not drink, but he had lit that large white pipe and nodded and smiled, and young Denia had thought: "My god, this is a cobra we deal with here this night."

Each young officer had tried to outdo the others in his commitment to the purity of the Communist revolution. Denia had been quiet. Then Stalin himself had pointed to him.

"And what do you think, quiet one?" Stalin had asked.

"I think everything they said is nice," Denia had said.

"Just nice?" Everyone had laughed. "Nice," the august chairman of the party had then said, "is a word for strawberries, not the revolution."

Denia had said nothing.

"Do you wish to change that word?"

"No," Denia had said.

His commander had become immediately uncomfortable, then had launched into a dialectical attack upon uncommitted revolutionaries conducting a bourgeois counterrevolution.

"And what do you think about that, young man?" Stalin had asked.

Young Denia had risen, because he knew he was dealing with his very life and he wanted to do it on his feet. He had also understood what his comrades had not, however. They too were dealing with their lives.

"What my commander says might be very true. I do not know. I am not a great professor, nor am I a great thinker. I know Russia needs a strong hand. Before the revolution, those who ruled ruled for their own privilege. There were hard times. Now there is a chance for a better life. That is good. It will not be easy to achieve. This is a big country. We are still backward. I am Russian. I know there will be much bloody work ahead. I know that for every thing done, there will be a thousand ideas of how to do it better. But I am Russian. I hold faith with the party. What they decide is their business. But in Gregory Denia, the party has a faithful servant."

The commander had attacked this position as being as serviceable for a czar, or for any other feudal leader, as for the Communist party. He asked why Denia had joined the party.

"Because our family was given three potatoes by a party member."

"For three potatoes you committed your life?" Stalin had asked.

"We were hungry, comrade chairman."

No one else in the room had noticed Stalin's eyes narrow ever so slightly, nor had they perceived that ever-so-slight nod. Gregory had been dismissed immediately by his superior. When he showed up the next morning at temporary headquarters in the remodeled Baptist Church, he found himself alone and wondered if headquarters had been moved. It hadn't. He was now commander, while still in his twenties. He never saw the others again, nor did he ask about them.

He had seen Stalin only once more, and that was during the early days of the great war, when Nazi troops roamed freely over western lands.

There had been a hundred officers of his rank

81

about to return to the field. He was organizing partisans behind the lines. Each officer had passed by Stalin and been introduced.

When it was Denia's turn, Stalin had smiled.

"Three potatoes," he had said.

"Three," had answered the then Colonel Denia.

A staff general had leaned over to explain some of Denia's recent heroic deeds. Stalin interrupted him with a brief wave of the hand.

"I know, I know," he had said. "The fiercest man on earth is a Russian with three potatoes in his belly."

It was a dirty war beyond anything seen since the barbaric hordes had slaughtered whole populations. To see what the Germans had done was beyond the hardness of even the NKVD. And then, of course, came the touchy stalking war with the west. Denia knew it would be a long one.

Three potatoes, he thought, as the Zil limousine moved quietly to the underground garage of the building on the square. He took a small elevator, one man only, to the codes room, and there he met a colonel in charge of one thing, a general in charge of another thing, and a half-dozen captains in charge of something else. There were maps and charts, and there were serious faces and people saluting all over the place and giving low-toned ominous warnings about this and that.

"Excuse me, gentlemen, I've got to pee," he said. "Go on with your briefing." He left the door open so he could hear everything they said. Some men turned their eyes away. Babies, he thought. Little ladies. The big bad KGB had turned into a bunch of little ladies.

He went back to the table.

"All right. Now I have heard about twenty reasons each of you is important to the survival of the state. But I have not been given any hard information. Let me give you two bits of hard information, five minutes apiece to think, and then we will do this all over again. One. My Treska unit is on the attack, mopping up against a defeated enemy. Therefore things do not go according to every little dot on every little piece of paper. You don't hear from people for weeks. That's all right. Secondly, what does Vassilivich say? He is the only worrier I respect."

No one waited five minutes. Vassilivich had not made his checks for three days. Auxiliary units had discovered the following men dead, they told him.

Denia listened to the long list. He took a red pencil from one of the officers standing over a map. He asked for the approximate times of the deaths, then he wrote in the times next to towns—Naples, Farfa, Athens, Rome.

"You said Ivan Mikhailov?"

"Yes, Major Mikhailov is dead."

"How?"

"Blunt instrument of some sort. Tremendous pressure."

"Of course. It would have to be," said Denia, remembering the incredible strength of the young giant. "Are you sure?"

"Yes. There was an autopsy. Major Mikhailov had enough rat poison in his veins to fell a battalion, but apparently it did not kill him."

"And no word from Vassilivich?"

"None."

Denia did not wish to express his suspicions at this moment, because things once said could never be brought back to safe silence—and who knew what any of these heel-clicking, saluting ladyniks would do.

"You're all jabbering about some great sudden assault by massive units, but I'll tell you something none of you has even mentioned yet. Look at my markings on the map. Look at the times. Look."

There was much talking about CIA backup teams, a rolling assault by multiple units, each going into action when the other had completed its mission.

One officer with an acne-ravaged face and sunken cheeks and thinning gray hair combed starkly to each side talked of a multinational chain reaction on isolated units. A conspiracy against Russia, possibly emanating from the Vatican.

Denia belched. He hadn't heard that sort of nonsense since a brief stopover in London, where British journalists had offered to sell any sort of story about anyone for a price.

An aide asked what the journalists meant.

"Would you like to read about America poisoning the Atlantic? The Israelis committing secret acts of war? The Danish government murdering children for cannibalism? The Dutch being secret racists? British journalism is the most lively money can buy. You name it and we'll write it. Books, of course, cost more than articles. But I guarantee, m'lord, there's nothing some of us can't write for a price. Want to read about the Pope's love affairs? His illegitimate children?"

"What love affairs? What illegitimate children?" the aide had asked.

"You pay for 'em and we'll write about 'em."

And this was all right for British journalism, but for serious men who dealt with life-and-death realities, it was appalling. So Denia belched, and he noticed an officer wince.

"Have any of you ever heard of an automobile?" asked Denia.

All the officers in the room without windows nodded that they had. A few cleared their throats. They avoided revealing glances at each other. Of course, they had heard of automobiles. What was the old man talking about?

"Can you all read wristwatches?" Denia asked.

Again the nods.

"Can you count?"

Yes, they could count. Would the most honored Marshal be more specific?

Denia put the red crayon on Rome.

"Imagine this red mark is a car. *Putt-putt-putt* goes the car. *Rrrrrr* goes the engine. Down this road, it goes *whooooossh*," said Denia. The pencil went from Rome to Naples. "Now we are in sunny Napoli. It is noon. Last night we were in Rome. Ah, here we go, we're heading north to Farfa. *Putt-putt-putt. Whoooosh. Vroom.* We are not even driving especially quickly. Now we go back to Rome and get on an airplane. It is a pretty airplane. It flies to Athens. *Wheeee. Vroooom. Whooosh.* Now it lands at Athens. What a pretty flight."

"Oh," said one officer who suddenly realized what Denia was talking about. Of course. They

85

had all been so involved in gigantic plots and multiple killer teams that no one had noticed one simple fact. The old warhorse had seen it at once.

"It's not a massive counterattack at all," said the young officer.

"Welcome to reality," said Marshal Denia.

"It's only one team. They went from one unit to another, of course. And undoubtedly that executive officer is helping them because he is the only one who is connected to the various teams. He has defected and is leading that killer team to each of our units," the young officer said.

"Wrong," said Denia loudly. "Absolutely wrong."

"Why?" said the young officer. Denia thought quickly. Something like this could get out of hand. And he had worked too long with Vassilivich to surrender the man to some Kremlin suspicion, where people slept cozily and safely and did not know what it was like to have someone put the barrel of a pistol to your belly and threaten to spread your insides into the nearest gutter.

"Because," said Denia.

"Because why, comrade marshal?" asked the officer.

"Because this is the way it was," he said, thinking clearly. "The Sunflower, our counterpart in the CIA, was becoming outmoded, obsolete. Why was it becoming obsolete? Because America had a much more effective killer team. What to do? What best way to take advantage of this new technique? Let our Treska expose itself by getting rid of what America would have to retire anyway. How to do this? Take away their weapons under the pretext of not wanting another international incident. Why else would Americans leave themselves defenseless? Is anyone here so stupid as to believe America would expose itself defenseless to this world?"

One officer thought America could be that stupid. He listed events of American foreign policy.

Denia said if the officer wanted to go to the Ministry of Foreign Affairs, he should do so. This was KGB.

"What Vassilivich has done, what this great and brilliant and courageous and loyal officer has done, is simply to save the party and the people of Russia. While ladyniks in the safety of the Dzerzhinsky Square building spin out fairy tales like Englishmen."

A liaison officer from the Red Navy took umbrage at being called English. Even being a marshal in the KGB did not give him the right to call another human being an Englishman.

"I am sorry your feelings are hurt. I only used English as a reference point. I did not even mean Englishman but English journalism as an example of silliness. I have great respect for the Red Navy and, it might surprise you, for the British Navy, and, it might surprise you even more, for most British. Now is everyone happy?"

The Naval officer accepted the apology.

"Good," said Denia and slapped the officer hard across the face. "Now, remember who I am. Marshal Denia who knows how to use his brains in combat, and yes, I do mean to insult every one of you—for not realizing that just as the Sunflower was obsolete for the Americans, so was the Treska unit for us. Because, you dummies, the Treska and the Sunflower were all but identical."

Stunned heads nodded. Even the officer whose right cheek was a red welt nodded. There was a reason why Denia was a leader of men, and now he was showing it.

"General Vassilivich is directing their new weapon against our Treska units, not to destroy us, but to offer up the lives of his comrades so we will be able to see what their new weapon is and counteract it. What he is doing is, granted, ruthless, but brilliant. We are taking one step backward to be able to take two forward. Gentlemen, America may have started this, but I tell you now, we will finish it."

He slammed his fist on the table.

"You have my life on it," he said with finality. "Keep your heads, ladyniks, and welcome to the world of the cold war."

He knew he did not have to add that his life depended on it. Of course it did. But it made a great dramatic impression just to say it. He was not as bold as the other officers might think. Massive failure of his units would probably mean death anyway, or something akin to it, like prison. And, calculating probabilities, Denia had decided that Vassilivich was either dead or doing exactly what Denia had said he was doing. All life was the edge of the sword.

Without those three potatoes, he might have starved to death anyway.

By 4:55 A.M. Moscow Time, Vassilivich, beautiful, intellectual Vassilivich, started justifying his commander's faith. A lower-rank consul in Athens had picked up a note thrown from a rented car. It was three words. Put together, they showed Vassilivich was alive and a captive.

By late afternoon of the next day, a Swedish unit had gotten a long note left outside a small chalet where the crushed bodies of the Gamma unit were found, their guns unfired, their knives still sheathed. Vassilivich was undoubtedly desperate. The note was handwritten on the back of five empty cigarette pack linings. It was not in code. It read:

D. New U.S. weapon. One man. Unusual abilities. What is Sinanju? Special methods. Giant trap. Treska units useless. One male, six feet tall, brown eyes, high cheekbones, thin, thick wrists, called Remo. Travels with Oriental who may be friend, teacher, poet? Called Chiun. Old. Sinanju the key. Long live sword and shield. V.

Denia called a special meeting in a room he had set up. More than a hundred officers from various branches of the KGB were present. He outlined the situation. There would be two steps: first, find out what this new unit was; second, destroy it. In those five shiny cigarette wrappers was the key. It was their job to unlock the puzzle, and Denia's job to wreak final revenge. The new unit designed to combat the American weapon would be named the Vassilivich group, in honor of Vassily Vassilivich, who was undoubtedly dead.

On the banks of the beautiful river Seine, Marshal Denia was being proven correct once again.

Vassilivich had himself broken the key of Sinanju. The Korean Chiun was one in a line of Masters of Sinanju that stretched back for untold centuries. If one took all the martial arts and traced their connections to each other and the history of the development of each, one might be able to calculate that perhaps all of them had come from a single source, most powerful at its center. Unlike television sets, martial arts became weaker as they became newer. There were no improvements in martial arts, only deteriorations, a slow dwindling away of essence, like radioactivity wearing out. The man Chiun was not a poet. It was even conceivable that he was more powerful than Remo.

Several times the comments "sun source" and "breathing" had been passed between the two in English. With breathing, these people were capable of harnessing the normal human body to its full potential. There was nothing miraculous about it at all. Moreover, if scientists ever got into the mysteries of Sinanju, they would probably discover how man had really survived on the ground before he organized into hunting parties and invented weapons. Barehanded man might at one time have been as strong as the sabretooth.

Sinanju, in some way, had harnessed normal human potential, which, interestingly, Vassilivich thought, brought up something from the old Christian religions. Christ had said it: you have eyes and do not see, ears and do not hear. Perhaps Christ had not been making a moral statement after all.

"Okay, fella, what are you writing?" asked Remo.

"Nothing," said Vassilivich.

"That's it for you," said Remo, and suddenly Vassilivich's eyes did not see, nor did his ears hear, nor did his body feel the Seine splash over him.

But it did not matter.

In the Dzerzhinsky Square building, Marshal Gregory Denia was getting the answers he wanted, and his tactical solution, he thought, was brilliant. If not biblical.

CHAPTER SIX

Ludmilla Tchernova noticed a blemish. Two inches below and slightly to the left of her left breast bloomed ever so slight a kiss of red on the immaculate, smooth white body. The breasts rose in youthful firmness, capped by mounds so perfectly round they looked as if they had been designed by a draftsman's compass. The waist narrowed in gentle tautness to creamy hips that billowed just enough to establish womanhood, and no more.

The neck was a graceful ivory pedestal for the crowning gem: the face of Ludmilla Tchernova.

She had the kind of exquisite face that made

other women want to go back to veils. When she entered a room, wives would kick husbands in the shins just to remind them they were still on earth. Her smile could get a rabid Communist to say mass on his knees. She made the average young Russian woman look like a tractor trailer.

She had violet eyes set in the perfection of a pale symmetry composed of a graceful nose and lips that looked as if they were almost artificial in their delicate pinkness. But that they were real showed when she smiled. Ludmilla Tchernova had fourteen different smiles. Her happiness and gentle-acquiescence smiles were her best. Her worst was the smile of sudden joy. She had been working on sudden joy for a month now, watching children when she gave them ice cream cones.

"Hello, dear, this is for you," she would say. And she would watch the child's lips carefully. Sudden joy tended to take two forms. One was a delayed action, which was very hard to get just right, and the other was an explosion of the lips, very wide. She could do the explosion, but, as she had told her uncle, who was a general on the Committee for State Security (KGB), it lacked force, and sometimes, if one looked closely, it could be misinterpreted as cruelty. She certainly did not want to look cruel when she intended to express sudden joy.

She had a major of the KGB, female, assigned to her. Lately this major had been picking up ice cream cones, cleaning the dirt off them, and handing them back to children. For as soon as Ludmilla had seen the smile she wanted, she tended to discard the cone.

"I'm not here to feed the masses," she had answered when the female major suggested that, with a little more effort, she might continue handing the ice cream cone forward until the child had a firm grasp on it. "I serve the party in a different way. If I wanted to feed children, I would have become a nurse. And it would be a waste of a great natural resource which I have chosen to give to the party and to the people."

"A little kindness cannot hurt," said the major, not especially known for a soft heart but who, in Ludmilla's presence, tended to think of herself as St. Francis of Assisi.

She was a relatively attractive Volga German with blond hair and blue eyes, clean features and an attractive body. Next to Ludmilla, she looked like a light heavyweight boxer at the end of his career. Ludmilla Tchernova could make a rainbow look plain.

Now there was a great problem, and as Ludmilla stared at the blemish beneath her left breast, she demanded of Major Natasha Krushenko what she had been fed the night before.

"Strawberries and fresh cream, Madame."

"And something else. There had to be something else." The voice was heavy with anger, but the face was calm. Grimaces could cause wrinkles.

"There was nothing else, Madame."

"There had to be to explain this blemish."

"The human body produces substances that create blemishes. It will disappear."

"Of course it will disappear. It's not your body."

"Madame, I have many blemishes like that."

"No doubt," said Ludmilla who had not been

listening to the answer but was very carefully outlining the blemish with her finger. She did not want to aggravate it more by touching it. She found it quite helpful to ignore the crudities of Major Krushenko. In the center of her entire world, this blemish on her body lounged in grievous and grating insolence. And that Krushenko lout claimed she hadn't even seen it at first. Krushenko was a barbarian.

She applied body cream made from Vitamin E, sardine innards, and bleached beet paste, and said a small prayer that this grief be removed from her life. Then she covered herself in a gauze bathrobe and packed her face with warm mud brought from the Caucusus.

It was in this manner, with her eyes closed, that she met with a marshal of the Soviet Socialist Republics, one of the highest-ranked KGB officials in the short history of the Communist state. Field Marshal Gregory Denia who had done something quite awesome in Western Europe, something which she had heard about during the gossip of the KGB community, and something which didn't interest her very much. It had to do with the Americans. But didn't everything? When it wasn't the Chinese or someone?

She did not open her eyes when she heard the clomping footsteps of the marshal in the hallway. Major Krushenko greeted the marshal and added congratulations for recent successes.

She heard him enter the sun room where she rested and plop his body heavily in a chair. She smelled the reek of cigars.

"Hello, Ludmilla," said Marshal Denia.

"Good afternoon, Gregory," said Ludmilla.

"I have come on business, my dear."

"And how is uncle Georgi?"

"Georgi is fine," Denia said.

"And Cousin Vladimir?"

"Vladimir is fine."

"And how are you?"

"I am fine, Ludmilla. We have an emergency and now you can repay to the state all that the state has given you. You can do for Mother Russia what armies cannot do, I believe. I am here to call on you to carry the banners of the heroes of Stalingrad and of your people, who will never again have to see their homes and their families brutalized."

"And how are you?" asked Ludmilla.

She heard a fist pound into the sofa on which she had heard Gregory lower himself. He expressed anger. He expressed hostility. He included a veiled threat and made accusations of a lack of gratitude to the state.

"Gregory, Gregory, of course I wish to help. I work for the same committee as you. Why do you show so much anger? You should be more like your executive officer, what's his name?"

"Vassilivich. General Vassily Vassilivich, dead in the line of duty, who has given his life so you may live here in safety where the capitalists cannot wring your neck."

"Yes, Vassilivich. That was his name. How is he?"

She felt the sudden shock of hands upon her very person. Rough palms rubbing off the soothing mud, thick brutal fingers at her neck. Denia was yelling at her.

"You will listen or I will shove your pretty face in a vat of acid. Damn your relatives. You will listen. My units lie strewn across the face of Europe and I am going to annihilate their killers. And you are going to help me or I will crush you."

Ludmilla shrieked, then cried, then begged for forgiveness, and vowed she would pay attention. Through her tears she asked to be allowed to get fully dressed. She was not prepared for this, she sobbed. She whimpered as Major Krushenko helped her, with a motherly arm, to one of her powder rooms.

Ludmilla thought she detected a small smile of triumph on Major Krushenko's plain face. Inside the powder room, the whimper disappeared. Ludmilla was crisp in her orders. She wanted a plain print dress without bra, a pair of light linen panties, and American cold cream.

She prepared herself in a record thirty-five minutes. She reintroduced tears to her eyes before she returned to the sun room.

Marshal Denia stood by one of the large windows, at a pre-boil, looking at his watch. But when he turned and saw the sweet freshness of Ludmilla's beauty and the rim of tears beneath her eyes, and when he heard her soft voice beg forgiveness, the anger vanished like air from a balloon. He nodded curtly.

She held his hands as he talked. He explained about the country's killer teams, and America's, how, after years of stalking, the heroes of the Soviet Socialist Republics had finally seen an opportunity to rid the continent of these murderers, and had struck back brilliantly and quickly.

Alas, it proved to be a trap by the cunning American mind. With the taste of victory in their mouths, the extended units of the peoples' teams, called Treska, had suffered a vicious onslaught by the capitalists, who were using a deadly team of but two men.

But Mother Russia had not bled for centuries to lower the standards of the people before gangsters. Russia was preparing its counterattack, which would be more victorious because of the greater obstacles to overcome.

The difficulties were, first the locating of so small a unit—two men at the most—second, finding out how they did what they did, what secret powers or tools they had. Once that was known, they could be annihilated, and the rightful dominance over intelligence in Europe would go to the superpower indigenous to Europe.

"Europe for the Europeans," said Ludmilla.

"Yes. Absolutely," said Denia, happy that Ludmilla was now listening. He wanted to kiss her beautiful cheeks, but he restrained himself by remembering all his men who were gone.

"And you want me to find out how they do what they do so we can defend ourselves. I can succeed where muscle cannot."

"Correct," said Marshal Denia, delighted.

"I am honored, gracious marshal." And she leaned over and kissed his rough, pudgy cheek, knowing that the neckline of her dress exposed her perfect breasts. She felt his arm reach around and ducked playfully under it.

"We have work now," she said with her "delightful" smile, a middle-range sort of thing used for refusing sexual overtures or a second slice of cake.

Laughingly she ushered him to the door. There would be problems of course. She did not want to have to fend men off until she reached her target man. That tired her so. When the door was shut behind Marshal Denia, Major Krushenko asked Ludmilla what had transpired. She knew they would be packing.

"Assholes got themselves killed and we have to bail them out," said Ludmilla.

"Oh," said Major Krushenko, with absolutely no surprise.

"Denia is in trouble and we're his long shot," said Ludmilla, who had known and understood KGB policy since childhood. Denia had always had a reputation for overextending himself, and, without that bookish Vassilivich to restrain him, he had undoubtedly gotten some of his people wiped out. Or captured. Or something. She hated the family business. It was so boring.

She repacked her face and re-oiled her body, and so spent the rest of the afternoon pleasantly, remaining gorgeous. The blemish was beginning to recede. She was going to be Delilah to America's Samson, whoever the lucky man was.

In America the President got the first good foreign news since the surrender of the Japanese in World War II. The Russian extermination squads known as Treska seemed to have abandoned aggressive activities in Western Europe. The news came from the Director of the Central Intelligence

Agency. The Secretary of State looked on. The President read the message and waited for the doctor to leave the Oval Office before commenting.

The Secretary of State said he hoped the cut on the President's forefinger would heal soon.

"Yes," said the President. "Those bandaids have very sharp edges and if you grab them wrong, they can cut like knives."

"Not as sharp as paper, though," said the CIA Director.

"You know," said the President, "the home is the most dangerous place of all. Seventy per cent of all accidents occur in the home."

The Secretary of State, in his urbane manner, decided cautiously and wisely not to ask the President why he had needed a bandaid. He saw a small bottle of burn ointment and an ice cube melting in an ashtray, and he did not want to hear that the President of the United States had burned himself on ice.

"Well, good news," said the President after the doctor left.

"We don't know why the Treska seems inoperative at this point in time, but they seem to have run into something that bloodied them pretty well," said the CIA Director.

"British, French, who?" asked the Secretary of State.

The CIA Director shrugged. "Who knows? They're not going to tell us anything until those Senate investigations quiet down. Who would want to trust us now?"

"Gentlemen," said the President, "it is neither the British nor the French, and I am not at liberty to say who or what it is, but as I told you at a recent meeting, this matter would be taken care of. And it has."

The Secretary of State wanted to know how. The President said there was no need for the Secretary to know. Nor was there a need for the Director of the CIA to know.

"Whatever did it, we're lucky it's on our side," said the CIA Director.

"And it will stay on our side as long as no one talks about it. Thank you for coming, gentlemen. Good day."

He eased the tight pressure of the bandaid on his finger, then looked up at the back of the Secretary of State.

"Uh, by the way, would you send the doctor back in, please? Thank you," said the President, hiding the new cut on his other hand.

In a three-star Paris hotel rated for its quality and service, Chiun decided to speak on the death of their guest of a few days, Vassily something with the funny name, the nice Russian boy.

He knew why Remo had killed the sweet, respectful young man.

"He was a KGB general, Little Father. He was the last of the Treska killers. That's what Smitty sent us over here to do."

Chiun slowly and precisely shook his head. His frail beard hardly moved with his head.

"No, that may be why Smith will believe you killed, but I know the true happiness you had."

"Happiness?" said Remo. He checked out the bathroom. The tub was much deeper than any in

101

America, and there was a sitting bowl that looked almost like a toilet, except it had two water faucet handles and a metal tube sticking up. It was for women. The hotel's name was Letutia. The ceilings were high, and the closets were not in the wall but separate dark wood pieces with legs. "Happiness?"

"Happiness," said Chiun.

"It was work," said Remo. "We went to the one known location of the Treska, grabbed a piece of it, and unraveled. Hey, you know how women use this thing?" Remo asked. He played with the faucet handles at the back of the almost toilet. He reasoned that it took some skill. The water went squirting up. A lot of skill.

"You enjoyed your work because the nice young Vassily showed proper respect. His teachers must have been very proud of him. He must have given them much joy, for in Russia they could say, this is my student and he has given me much joy. Not like in some other countries where those who give the greatest knowledge are abused and ignored and generally discarded."

"What is wrong?" asked Remo.

"When I recited Ung Poetry to you, you merely left the room."

"I never heard of Ung Poetry."

"Of course. Like diamonds thrown into mud before the worm. The worm slithers over great beauty as but a sharp obstacle. You never heard because you never listened. You do not know languages or kings. You do not know the names of the Masters of Sinanju in their proper order, or who begat whom. You were eating animal fat meats on soft decayed bread when I found you, and you do not know who is where or what is why, but rumble along in your dark cloud of ignorance."

"I listen. I've been training more than ten years now. I do what you tell me. I think like you tell me. Sometimes I'm beginning to think I am you. Everything you say I respect. This is so. I have never gone against you."

"Then let us do honor to the Masters of Sinanju. We will start with the first Master who came from the caves of the mist."

"Almost everything," said Remo, who remembered some of the early sessions where he had tried to get down who was whose father and who was whose mother, and they had all sounded overbearingly repetitious and unimportant. At that time, Chiun had said that Remo could not learn, because his training was starting too late in life.

"Vassilivich would have learned," said Chiun. "He was a good boy. In my history of my mastership, I shall call myself 'teacher of the ungrateful.'"

Remo turned on the television set. It jutted out of the wall on a platform just above his head. There was a picture of Charles De Gaulle talking. It was a film of his life. He did not understand French. Chiun did.

If Chiun's baggage had not been misplaced in shipping, Chiun would have had his own television programs which he could run on tape. Lately, however, he had been looking mostly at reruns. America, he said, had desecrated its own pure art form, turning it into filth and violence and the reality of everyday life. After that, Remo could not convince

Chiun that every American family did not harbor in its midst a dope addict, a child beater, a leukemia victim, a crooked mayor, and a daughter who'd had an abortion.

Chiun looked at De Gaulle's image and told Remo to turn off the television. "There was never any work from that man," he said. "Now the Bourbon kings, ah, they knew how to employ an assassin. France was always a good place until the animals took over." Chiun shook his head sadly. He sat in the middle of the floor on the soft brown carpeting before the two large beds. By "animals taking over," Chiun meant the French Revolution of 1789. Every French president after that remained to Chiun a wide-eyed radical.

"I give up," said Remo. "When did I fail to properly listen to your Ung poetry? I never heard it."

"I was reciting it to that nice Vassilivich boy."

"Oh, that stuff," Remo said. "I don't understand Ung."

"Neither does the carpet or the wood of the closets," said Chiun. With a great sigh, he said he must now explain Paris to Remo, only praying that Remo would remember some of what he had been told.

Downstairs in the lobby of the Letutia, Chiun had a small argument with the concierge about something. Chiun silenced him with a word.

Remo asked what the argument was about.

"If you understood French, you would know," Chiun said.

"Well, I don't understand French."

"Then you do not know," said Chiun as if that pleasantly explained it all.

"But I want to know," said Remo.

"Then learn French," said Chiun. "Real French, not the garbage spoken today."

The street was the Boulevard Raspail. Two elderly woman sold sweets and crèpes in a small white stall on a corner. A man in a dark limousine did a quick double take on Remo and Chiun. The car pulled over to the curb across the intersection. Remo saw the man lift a small camera to the back window. Remo did not recognize the man but the man obviously was looking for someone who looked like them.

By the time they had walked across one of the graceful wide bridges that spanned the dark Seine, Remo knew the confusion had ended. There were two tails, both young men, following, and three more staked out on the far side of the bridge. It was not hard to tell a tail, because he locked into your rhythms instead of his own.

A tail could be reading a newspaper, looking at a river, or gazing at the outside of the mangificent Louvre that Remo and Chiun now were approaching. No matter what he was doing, he was really locked with you. Eyes did not focus properly, or something. Remo could not quite explain it. He had tried once to tell Smith about it, but he had fallen back on "you just know."

"But how do you know?" Smith had asked.

"When a person really reads a newspaper, he does things differently."

"But what?"

"I don't know. It's different. Like right now, I

know I only have part of your mind. Most people can't hold a single thought for more than a second. Minds are jumpy. But a tail has to keep his mind still. I don't know. Just take my word for it. You can tell."

So it was spring in Paris, and Remo caught a couple of smiles from a couple of beautiful women, and he returned them, but in such a way as to acknowledge their loveliness but decline their invitation.

Chiun called this a typical American-sex-fiend way of looking at things. He too noticed the tails. But as they approached the Louvre, and as Chiun looked into a window, he emitted a low wail.

"Ung poetry, Little Father?"

"No," said Chiun. "What have they done to the Louvre? What have they done? The animals!" Chiun covered his eyes. He made a fast check with marks on the bends of the River Seine, repeating all the descriptions given in the history of Sinanju, and yes, it was the place, and the animals that had followed the Bourbons had crassly turned the place into a museum.

People even had to pay to enter now. What disgust.

Remo saw the gilt ceilings, the rococo marble, the paint on paint, and he thought, "If this weren't the world-famous museum, it would be in bad taste." It was just too much. Chiun shuffled through the crowds, checking one spacious room after another. Here a prince had slept. Here the king had entertained briefly. Here was where the king's advisors had held councils of war and peace. Here a great festival had been held. Here was where the king's mistress had slept. Here the Count de Ville had planned to assassinate the king. And what had they done? That had not only remodeled the beautiful palace—one of the true art forms of the world, like American dramas used to be—but they had strewn the whole place with ugly pictures and statues. Garbage. The animals had turned the palace into a garbage heap.

Chiun slapped a gendarme who was so surprised by the little Oriental that he merely blinked.

"Animals," shrieked Chiun. "Degenerate animals." They had not only destroyed a palace, they had made a chapter of the history of Sinanju obsolete. Chiun had always wanted to see Paris, especially for this palace so well described by his ancestors, but now the mobs had ruined it.

"What mobs?" asked Remo.

"Everyone after Louis the Fourteenth." And even he, according to Chiun, had not been all that gracious. He confided to Remo that he was glad Charles the Fifth was not alive to see it now.

A prim nun in a gray suit and a short black bonnet led a line of well-scrubbed little girls with blue blazers and school emblems, carrying small locked briefcases. They pattered down the hall like cute, prim ducks in a row.

"Barbarians," Chiun yelled at them. "Brutal barbaric animals." The nun placed herself between her students and the yelling Chiun and quickly herded them down the well-lit hall.

"Vicious degenerates," Chiun said. The tails appeared at the end of the hall, their faces pointed to pictures implacably, as if attached by strings.

"I've got work to do, Little Father. Can I get some privacy in this place?"

"Yes," said Chiun. Three rooms from the Mona Lisa there was a pink marble wall along which Chiun counted marble ornaments. At the count of eight, he raised a long fingernail chest high and part of the wall swung open. So graceful was the craftsmanship that the opened wall did no look like some intrusion of a secret passage, but just another room. This one, however, was without lights. It smelled of dusty death and had walls of rough rock. Remo beckoned to the two tails, and with a bit more surprise than the average stranger beckoned to by someone, they came. Remo's hands shot out like the quick snap of a frog's tongue and the two went smashing into the rough rock floor of the secret room. The wall closed behind all four.

One had his hand on a small caliber pistol in an ankle holster. He had his hand on it only briefly, as Remo blended all of it into a painful bloody mess with his right shoe.

Without too much pressure against their spines, the men talked profusely. Unfortunately, they talked neither in English nor Korean, the only two languages Remo spoke in. He needed Chiun to translate.

A small light diffused into the room from above, making the room look as if it were in eternal dusk. Remo noticed a dry skeleton with a small hole in its temple, sitting against the rock wall as if it were a beggar waiting for a cup to be filled with coins.

Remo asked Chiun to translate for him. Chiun said he was hired as an assassin, not a language teacher. Remo said it was part of the work. Chiun

108

said it was never agreed to with Smith that his duties included translating. He complained that Smith had promised to send him tapes of the soap operas but that they had not come yet. The tail who still had two good wrists and two good ankles went for a shoulder holster. Remo put a knuckle into his sternum. Part of a ventricle came out of his mouth like spit.

"Now we have only one, Little Father. Will you please help? Just find out who they are and why the tail."

Chiun said it would dishonor his ancestors to act as a language teacher, especially in this very room where the Count de Ville's body was.

"As a favor to me?" Remo asked.

Chiun agreed but noted it would be one more favor to be unrepaid. He said there was a point at which generosity ceased and abuse began. That point had been passed eight years before. Nevertheless his good heart prevailed. He questioned the man, who lay in pain. Then he ended the pain with eternal finality.

It was Remo's job to stack the two bodies neatly next to the skeleton. Remo said he would do it and thanked Chiun. What did the man say?

Chiun said he had been asked to question him, not repeat the answers. Repeating answers was something else.

Remo said that repeating answers was part of translating. Chiun said if Remo wanted that he should have asked for that also. Remo saw the hole in the skull of the skeleton was a bit too wide. He remarked that Chiun's ancestor had been sloppy or getting old, because he had mashed the skull instead of penetrating it sharply.

Chiun said that Remo's ancestors had probably fought with rocks, and that Remo was probably the first who knew how to breathe. Besides, Remo didn't even know his ancestors.

Remo said he didn't even know his father and only remembered the orphanage. Which was one of the reasons CURE had chosen him in the first place. He had no known relatives.

Chiun said if that was an attempt to make him feel guilty, it had failed miserably.

"Miserably."

Remo said it wasn't an attempt to make Chiun feel guilty. It was a fact. Chiun was the one who tried to make people feel guilty.

In the administration offices of the Louvre, there was chaos that afternoon. Voices were coming from the walls all over the museum. At first, it was thought that someone had brought in a television set. Then it was thought that a tape recorder with American voices had been placed somewhere. Guards scurried up and down the corridors looking for the exact sources of the resonating voices talking about guilt and orphanages and failure.

Visitors from all over the world, many who had come to this city just to visit this museum, stared at one another.

Then suddenly the voices stopped and there was incredible silence in the vast museum, for everyone had been quiet trying to pick out the strange sounds.

A nun ran horrified to a gendarme. Two men, one an Oriental, had emerged from a wall in the

Cour Carée section. The wall had shut after them. The Oriental had started the girls crying because he had called them vicious animals. He was arguing with the white man. Most of the talking was in English. The white man was saying he was sorry for asking for a simple favor.

When the guard returned with the assistant director of the museum, they could find no opening in a wall. The nun was put under sedation. Gendarmes escorted the girls back to their school.

And outside, walking to the hotel, Remo dismissed all Chiun was saying.

"I'm not interested in the last time Wang or Hung saw Paris." He stared at Chiun. "I just asked a simple little favor. I'm never going to ask again."

But Chiun wouldn't tell Remo what the tail had said.

Remo said he didn't care.

Chiun asked why, if Remo didn't care, did he have Chiun do the work of the translator? The problem, Chiun said, was that he was too easy-going. People tended to walk all over the good-hearted.

The next morning, Remo met the most beautiful woman he had ever seen.

CHAPTER SEVEN

It was midnight and only a man of peculiar habits would be working at his desk, so Dr. Harold W. Smith was at his when the special telephone rang.

When he picked it up, the first thing he heard was the receiver dropped on the other end of the call. There was a moment's fumbling, and then the President's voice came on in a rough-edged whisper, competing with a raucous background squawk.

"Good work."

"Sir?" said Smith.

"The European business. Went like a charm. I hear Treska's just about out of business."

"I can hardly hear you," Smith said.

"Well, somebody's here," the President hissed.

"Who?"

"Big Mama. The First Lady. She set her CB radio up in here."

"Mister President. In a dozen years this has never happened. If you wish to speak to me, I suggest you do it when no one else is around."

"How do I get rid of Big Mama?"

"Push her through the door and lock it behind her," Smith said, and hung up. After a few minutes, the phone rang again.

"Yes?" Smith said.

"You didn't have to get huffy," said the President in his normal voice, a voice that would be at home on a Detroit assembly line or pumping gas in Joliet, the kind of voice that belonged to a man people would elect and elect and elect to most offices because he was one of them. It was also the kind of voice that people voted against for the highest office in the land because it was too much like "one of them," and they wanted a President who was better than they were. And sounded it.

"I'm sorry you feel that way, Mr. President," Smith said, "but for more than a dozen years I have maintained this unit's security and secrecy. I haven't done it by playing 'breaker, breaker, there's a picture taker' on the radio with my wife in the room."

"Well, all right. Anyway, it looks like those two cleaned up everything in Europe. Reports I get say the Russians have withdrawn all their Treska units."

"Your reports are wrong."

"Wrong? I can hardly believe that. This is what we've heard from friendly nations. Allies."

"Wrong," said Smith. "The Treska hasn't been called home; it's been destroyed. There is no more Treska in the field."

"You mean . . . ?"

"I mean just that. There was an assignment to neutralize the Treska and render it harmless. They have been rendered the most harmless they can be," Smith said.

"Those two?"

"Those two," Smith said. "But it is not over. There is a Marshal Denia who has been called back to the Kremlin for discussions. He is in charge of Treska. He will be back at us with something new."

"What should we do?" the President asked.

"Leave it to us. The situation will be handled."

"Well . . . if you think so. . . ." The President seemed reluctant.

"Good night," Smith said abruptly.

After replacing the phone inside his desk drawer, Smith sat reading copies of new reports produced by CURE's overseas agents—policemen, newspapermen, minor foreign officials, all of whom knew only that they provided information to some agency of the U.S. for a monthly check. All of them "knew" it was the CIA. And they were all wrong.

Their reports, raw information, some of it solid, some of it not better than rumor or outright lies from those who were taking money from Russia to ship America false information, came pouring into CURE's computers at Folcroft Sanitarium in Rye,

New York, on the shores of Long Island Sound. There it was mixed and matched in a way no single human mind could emulate. A man missing from his usual office for a week, a body found floating in a river somewhere, an airline ticket bought and paid for in cash by a man with a Russian accent—the computers put all the tiny threads of fact and information together, and then, on a console that only Dr. Smith could operate, wove out for him what had happened, classifying its results Conclusive, Highly Probable, Probable, Possible, Unlikely and Impossible.

Then Smith, after using a computer to do work a man could not do, did what a computer could never do. He made instant judgments, weighing risks and rewards, conflicting priorities, money and manpower problems, to spell out CURE's next assignment. He did it day in and day out with few mistakes, aware of but never awed by the fact that the only thing that stood between a strong United States and a United States exposed naked and defenseless before its enemies in the world was Dr. Harold W. Smith. And Remo. And Chiun.

Smith was not awed because he lacked the imagination to be awed. It was his greatest liability as a human being, and in turn his greatest asset as the head of a secret agency that had suddenly been given the global job of defending America.

"That Smith is an idiot," Chiun said.

"What now, Little Father?" Remo asked patiently, watching Chiun who wore his golden morning robe but was visible only in black silhouette against the bright early morning sunlight pouring through their triple-width hotel windows. Chiun looked out over the street. He was absolutely motionless, his hands extended straight out in front of him, his long-nailed fingers pointing ahead, near but not touching the thin yellow gauze draperies that hung from ceiling to floor.

"We are done here," Chiun said. "So why are we still here? This is a city where every food is smothered in sauce, every juice is fermented, and the people speak a tongue that grates upon the eardrums like a file. And then, what they allowed to happen to the Louvre. The shame of it. I do not like France. I do not like Frenchmen. I do not like the French language."

"You prefer to hear Americans speak English?" Remo asked.

"Yes," Chiun said. "Just as I would prefer to hear any other kind of donkey bray."

"We'll be going home soon."

"No. We will be going back to the land of Smith and that maker of automobiles. For you and for me, our home is Sinanju."

"Don't start that again, Chiun," said Remo. "I've been there. Sinanju is cold, barren, heartless and treacherous. It makes Newark look like heaven."

"How like a native to speak disparagingly of the land he loves," Chiun said. "You are of Sinanju." While he spoke, his fingers had not moved a fraction of an inch. In silhouette, he looked like a plaster statue of Jesus as shepherd.

Remo had stared at the Oriental's fingertips, eyes sharper than a hawk's, trying to see even the faintest quiver of motion, the slightest tensing of a muscle pushed beyond its limit of endurance, a twitch, a tic, but he saw nothing, only ten long fingers extended, at arm's length, an inch away from yellow drapes that hung perfectly straight, perfectly still, from ceiling to floor.

"I am an American," Remo said.

"Rooty toot toot," Chiun said. Remo started to laugh, then stopped when he saw the curtains move. Slowly, their delicate weight seeming to move, massively, like an ice age crossing a continent. The curtains moved slowly forward, a full inch, until they touched Chiun's extended fingertips, and then they swung forward even more until his fingertips were surrounded by the thin gauze which wrapped itself around the tips of his fingers as if they were iron filings and his fingers were magnets.

Chiun dropped his hands to his sides and the drapes retreated, swinging softly back into place.

The old man turned and saw Remo staring at him.

"Enough," he said, "for one day. Let that be a lesson to you. Even the Master must exercise."

The drapes were again motionless.

"Do that again," Remo said.

"Do what?"

"That thing with the curtains."

"I just did it," Chiun said.

"I want to see how you did it."

"You were watching. You did not see before. How will you see if I do it again?"

"I know how you did it. You inhaled and the drapes came to you."

117

"I inhaled with my fingers?" asked Chiun.

"How?" said Remo.

"I spoke French to it. Very softly so you would not hear. Even drapes understand French because it is not a hard language, even if they garble the pronunciation."

"Dammit, Chiun, I'm a Master of Sinanju too. You've told me that. You shouldn't withhold information from me. How am I going to support the village when I take over from you? How are all those sweet people I've come to know and love, how are they going to live if I can't ship them the gold? How can I do that if I can't even make a curtain lift?"

"You promise then?"

"Promise what?" asked Remo suspiciously. He had the vague sense that he was being pulled into Chiun like the drapes.

"To send the tribute to the village. To feed the poor, the elderly, the infants. For Sinanju is a poor village, you know. In bad times, we. . . ."

"All right. All right. All right. I promise, promise, promise, promise. Now how'd you do that with the curtain?"

"I willed it."

"You willed it? And just like that, it happened? Remo asked.

"Yes. I have told you many times that all life is force. You must work to extend that force beyond the thin shell which is your skin. Extend that force beyond your body, and then objects that fall into the field of that force can be controlled by it."

"Okay, you've told me what, now tell me how."

"If you do not know the what, you cannot do the how."

"I know the what," Remo said.

"Then you can already do the how. No one need show you," said Chiun.

"A typical non-answer," Remo said.

"You must practice," Chiun said. "Then you will be able to do it too. You had better start soon because you're not going to have me to kick around much longer."

"Oh? Where are you going?"

"I am retiring. I have a little sum put by which will enable me to live out my few remaining years in dignity. In my home village. Respected. Honored. Loved."

"Don't give me that. The last time you were home, the village sent a tank after you," Remo said.

"An error," Chiun said. "Never to be repeated. I have advice for you, regarding your future duties as Master of Sinanju."

"Yeah?"

"Yes. Do not take any checks. Make sure the tribute to the village is in gold. Remember. I will be there to inspect it when it comes And I do not trust Smith. He is an idiot, that man."

"Anything else?"

"Yes. Practice."

"Practice what?" Remo asked.

"Everything," Chiun said. "You do it all so badly."

"Little Father," Remo said, standing in the center of the room. "Ragaroo, digalee, freebee doan."

"What is that?"

"It's an old American art form called Mung Poetry. You know what it means?"

"No. What, if anything?"

"Go blow it out your ears," Remo said and walked out of the hotel room.

Entering the lobby, Remo took one step off the elevator and stopped cold, as if he had just remembered he had forgotten to put on his pants.

From across the Persian-rugged lobby a woman smiled at him. She was long-legged and dark-haired. She wore a white silk pants suit, its jacket tied loosely above her hips with a belt, and even though she lounged on a chair, Remo knew that when she stood up the garment would be unwrinkled. She was a woman on whom a wrinkle, either of flesh or fabric, would have seemed like the defacing of a monument.

She stood and opened her arms wide as if welcoming Remo to step into them. Her long eyelashes flickered. Her eyes were gentian violet, made even more violet by the light blue of her upper lids, a light blue that seemed a gift of nature and not of a colorist's brush.

Remo moved forward dully across the lobby, toward the woman whose eyes were fixed on him with the unblinking gaze of a cheetah on the hunt. He felt ten years of Sinanju slip away from him. Ten years of control of mind and body so specific, so rigid, so detailed, that even his sex drive had turned into a physical exercise and an excuse to practice techniques. But as slowly as it had gone, that quickly it had returned, and Remo was consumed with the thought of the dark-haired woman who still stood, smiling at him.

He stumbled across the lobby toward her out-stretched arms, feeling foolish, wondering what he would do if those arms were not open for him, wondering what he would do if, at the last minute, she looked past him, stepped by him and swept some other man into her arms.

He knew what he would do. He would kill the other man. He would kill him on the spot, immediately, without remorse or feeling, and then he would grab the woman and drag her from the hotel and take her to a safe place from which she would never leave him.

When he neared her, the woman's arms dropped and like a chastened schoolboy, Remo stopped short.

He swallowed hard.

He tried to smile and even as it lit on his face, he knew it was a lopsided, sheepish smirk.

"My name is . . ."

"Your name is Remo," the woman said coldly. "You are an American. My name is Ludmilla. I am a Russian. I do not like Americans. You are decadent."

"Never more so than now," Remo said. "Why did you stand with your arms open?"

"Because I wanted to show you your foolish stupid decadence so that you would know the kind of idiot you are; the kind of imbecile I could make of you."

She walked away from Remo toward the door of the hotel. The bellboy scurried ahead of her to open the door, even though it was automatic and opened electronically when someone stepped on the rubber-matted approach plate.

"Wait," Remo called, but the woman was gone out into the street, her very back exuding disdain for Remo. He ran to the door. It was the entrance door and the mechanical opener would not work from his side of the lobby. He used his right hand to teach it nèver again to stop anybody who was in a hurry to leave.

The woman was getting into a cab. The doorman went to close it after her. Gently. She was not the kind of woman after whom one slammed cab doors, even if she had not given him a tip. She had looked at him and almost smiled; it would last him the rest of the day.

Something stopped the cab door from closing. The doorman pushed harder.

"Just a minute," Remo said. He pulled the door open, extricated his left foot, then slid into the back seat of the cab and closed the door himself.

"Presumptuous bumpkin," the woman said.

"None other," said Remo. "Driver, take us anywhere at all, just as long as it takes a long time."

The driver turned. "Madame?" he said.

"Drive, I said," Remo ordered.

The driver nodded as if he was the creator and preserver of a unique moment in the history of old world charm, when actually he was wondering what kind of tip he would get out of this ride. Good-looking women rarely tipped cabdrivers in Paris. And this American didn't look like a tipping tourist either.

When the cabdriver pulled away from the curb, Ludmilla said to Remo: "What do you want of me?"

"No. What do you want of me?"

"To be left alone. You can start now."

"Do you dislike all Americans equally? Or is it just me?"

"It is just you," Ludmilla said.

"Why?"

"Because you are an American spy, a killer, a . . ."

"Wait a minute." Remo leaned over the seat until his mouth was close to the driver's right ear. He reached up his hands and touched the bony prominences behind and below each ear. He pressed slightly as he said, "Just for a while, I'm going to do something to your ears."

The driver turned and in heavily accented English said, "I can't hear you. Something is wrong with my ears."

Remo made the okay sign and sat back. The driver continued rubbing, first his right ear, then his left, trying to restore his hearing.

"You were saying?"

"You are an American spy, a killer, a brute."

"And you?" Remo asked.

"I am the Russia spy who has come to kill you."

"Do I get my choice of ways to die?" Remo asked. " 'Cause I've got some great ideas."

"Only if the way is slow and painful," Ludmilla Tchernova said.

"Definitely slow," Remo said. "But I'm not much on pain."

"Too bad, American. Pain is definitely on your agenda."

"Why aren't you afraid of me?" Remo asked.

Ludmilla took a deep breath that noisily rustled the shiny fabric of her suit. Even sitting, the suit pulled tight against the curves of her body. She was so perfect she did not seem normal.

"You Americans are all fools," she repeated. "You will never hurt a woman. Cowboy mentality. I have seen all the movies."

"I've killed women," Remo said casually.

"That is because you are an indiscriminate slaughterer," Ludmilla said. "All Americans are. Remember Vietnam. Remember John Waynes. Remember Gene Autries. Remember Clint Westwood."

"All right," said Remo," now that I know you hate me and you're going to kill me, do I get a last request?"

"Only if it is not offensive to the state."

Breakfast, it was decided, was not offensive to the state, and Remo told the driver to stop at the nearest café.

The driver kept going until Remo leaned forward and made twisting pressures with his thumbs behind the driver's ears. The driver's face brightened as his hearing returned and he suddenly heard the noisy honking of Paris morning traffic, the most unruly morning traffic of all cities, the traffic noise of a populace with a hangover.

"Stop here," Remo repeated.

He and Ludmilla ate breakfast at a streetside café under a bright umbrella that was the finest umbrella Remo had ever seen, at a table with a dirty tablecloth that was the finest dirty tablecloth Remo had ever seen, under a bright morning sun which Gallic ingenuity had arranged at just such an angle that it shone under all the umbrellas into all the diners' eyes, and which Remo decided, after much reflection, was just the finest bright morning sun he had ever had shining in his eyes, blinding him.

Unlike most Russian visitors to Western countries who gorged themselves with food as if Russia was just a vast empty icebox, Ludmilla ate only fruits with cream. Remo sipped Vichy water and picked at steamed brussels sprouts.

"Here, American," Ludmilla said, pushing a strawberry at Remo. "Try one."

"No, thank you."

"You do not have these in America," she challenged.

"Yes, but I do not eat them."

"An egg, then? I will order you an egg."

"No eggs."

"Aha, you do not eat strawberries and you do not eat eggs. Is this your secret?"

"What secret?"

"The secret of your power to overcome some of our best men," Ludmilla said.

"No."

"Oh," she said, and put the strawberry back into her own mouth.

"It is the Vichy water," she said.

Remo shook his head.

"Then what is your secret?"

"Clean living, clean thoughts, and pure motives. Not like those two friends of yours across the street."

"Where?" she said, looking surprised with a smile. It was one of the fourteen smiles she had down perfectly—honest surprise.

125

"Over there." Remo nodded his head toward his right shoulder.

Across the narrow sidestreet stood two men wearing heavy blue serge suits that bagged at the knees. They also wore brown shoes, white shirts, and black ties. Each wore a hat equipped with—as a conciliatory gesture to Parisian fashion and decadence—a small red feather in the brim.

Ludmilla looked them over as if she were a butcher inspecting a hindquarter that had turned suspiciously green.

"They are gross," she said.

The two men stared back stolidly at the staring Remo and Ludmilla until they apparently discerned that they were the watchees and not the watchers and they began to shuffle their feet, light cigarettes, and stare at nonexistent overhead planes.

"I thought their disguises were wonderful," Remo said. "Who'd ever suspect they weren't Parisians?"

Ludmilla threw back her head and laughed. It was another of her fourteen perfections—a smiling laugh of wild abandon. Remo fell deeper in love, and he fell deeper still when he saw the long line of her swanlike but strong throat, as her head reached back and laughed toward the sky.

When the check came, Ludmilla insisted upon paying it. "Mother Russia does not take charity," she told Remo with a knowing lift of her eyebrows. She did not tell him that it was the first check she had ever picked up in her life.

She carefully counted out French franc notes and put them into the hand of the hovering waiter who, even in the morning, was dressed in a tuxedo and carried a silver tip plate.

"There," she said, looking at the man. "That is enough."

"Surely Madame has forgotten something," he said, looking at the bills.

"No. Madame has forgotten nothing."

"But surely, a tip?"

"There is no tip," Ludmilla said. "A waiter gets paid to wait. He gets paid by his employer, not by his customer. Why should I pay you an amount your employer does not think you are worth paying himself?"

"It is difficult to eat on a waiter's salary," the man said, still trying to smile, but his lips were pulled tightly across his teeth.

"If you wanted to be rich, perhaps you should have found some other career than being a waiter," Ludmilla suggested.

The man's eyes narrowed but the smile never wavered. "Ah, yes. But I was the wrong sex to be a courtesan."

"Keep trying, pal. You may make it yet," Remo said, standing.

"Perhaps Monsieur has something for me," the waiter tried.

Remo nodded. He picked something up from the table next to his. The waiter extended his always open, always hungry hand, palm up.

Remo ground out a cigarette on his hand. "How's that?" he said.

The waiter yelled.

Remo said, "Tell Lafayette we were here."

He walked off after Ludmilla. She did not walk, he noticed, like most Russian revolutionaries, who always seemed to have two problems: their pants were on fire, and they were trying to beat to the nearest corner a bus that traveled with the speed of light. Ludmilla strolled like a young woman in Paris intent on giving as much as possible of the world a chance to see her.

"Before I have to kill you," she said to Remo, "I will give you the chance. Return with me to Russia. I will put in the good word for you."

"No," said Remo. "Counter-offer. You come with me to America."

Ludmilla shook her head. "It is a land of many beauties, your America. I have seen your women, your actresses and singers. They are most beautiful. Who would even see me?"

"You're a star that would shine in any heaven," Remo said.

"Yes," said Ludmilla, quickly converted to a point of view she had held all along anyway.

They walked along in silence and Remo listened to Paris. With the end of the morning rush hour traffic, the city hummed, a dull throbbing sound almost below the level of perception, but numbing the brain and senses. New York was noisy; it was a city where someone was always shouting. Paris was a city in which everyone was whispering at once, and no one was listening.

Except Remo. And out of the hum and the buzz he picked out what he wanted: the heavy clump and click of the two Russians following him and Ludmilla.

"They're still following us," Remo said.

"Oh, those swine. They never leave one alone," Ludmilla said. "I wish they were dead."

"The wish is father to the dead," Remo said. He grabbed Ludmilla's elbow and steered her gently into an alley.

"What does that mean?" she said.

"Damned if I know," said Remo.

They were in a narrow dead end, only a half-block long. It was bordered on both sides and at the end by three-story-high buildings that people called slums in the United States but called quaint when they arrived in Paris on a vacation to get away from the American slums.

Remo stood Ludmilla against the powdery brick wall of a building and walked across the cobblestone street to wait. There were no cars on the little alley.

The two men turned the corner, looking into the alley, then stopped. Remo winked at Ludmilla. She was looking at the two men and Remo saw her nod slightly to them. They came forward toward Remo, their hands jammed into their jacket pockets, their metal-tipped heels clicking like castanets on the stones of the street.

Ludmilla fished in her gold brocade bag for a gold cigarette case. She flipped it open and extracted one cigarette, a long golden holder, and a thin golden lighter, and began assembling her smoke. A Russian scientist had reported that cigarette smoke caused the skin to age prematurely. From that day on, Ludmilla had used the long holder to keep the cigarette flame away from her face.

She watched as the men approached and stood

in front of Remo, who leaned casually against the stone wall of a building.

"You are a killer," said one of them, a short stocky man with a face as memorable as a well-worn patio block.

"Actually, I'm a dancer," Remo said. "If it was raining, I'd give you 'Singing in the Rain'" He looked skyward and shrugged. "Not even a drizzle."

"You have killed many of our men," said the other man, a human built generally along the lines of a refrigerator.

"Right," said Remo, "so two more won't make any difference."

The two men pulled their hands from their pockets. Guns were in their hands

Remo pulled their guns from their hands and then their hands from their arms and then put the two of them into the stone wall where their heads hit with matching clunks and became two more ringing endorsements of the poster there proclaiming Liberté, Egalité, Fraternité.

Ludmilla was about to flick the cigarette lighter when she heard the two men's heads hit and looked up to see them become part of the beauty that was Paris.

She ran across the street to Remo who was putting the men's guns into a sewer.

"Oh, I was so worried."

"Yeah," said Remo taking her arm and leading her back toward the main street. "I want to talk to you about that."

"About what?"

"Look, these dingoes come into the alley and

you give them the high sign to go get me. Now if you're going to keep trying to kill me, it's going to be difficult to have any kind of meaningful relationship."

"It is true," Ludmilla said. She hung her head, doing abject sorrow.

"So what are we going to do?" Remo asked. "Seeing as how we're in love."

Ludmilla looked up brightly. "Suppose I only try to kill you on Mondays, Wednesdays, and Fridays?"

Remo shook his head. "Naah, it'll never work. Too complicated. I have trouble remembering days and things."

Ludmilla nodded, understanding fully the immensity of that problem.

"You understand," she said, "that the only reason these people came after you was so that I could see you in action."

"I figured something like that."

"So I could learn your secret," she said.

"Right."

"You are awesome."

"Well, when I'm at my peak, I'm pretty good," Remo allowed. "Look." He stopped on the street and faced the young Russian woman, taking her elbows in his hands. "Just what is your mission? Is it to kill me or find out how I work?"

"Find out how you work. Then others can kill you."

"Okay, then it's solved. You do anything to try to find out how I work. But don't try to kill me. Fair?"

131

"I have to think about it," she said. "It may be just a dirty capitalist trick to try to stay alive."

"Trust me," Remo said, looking hard into her violet eyes with a look that had never failed before.

"I trust you, Remo," the woman said. "I will not try to kill you."

"Okay, then that's settled."

"But others might," Ludmilla said. It was not a prediction, it was an insistence. She would not enter into this pact with Remo unless other Russians had the right to try to kill him. After all, what did Remo take her for? A coat-turn?

"I don't care who else tries to kill me. I just don't want you trying it."

"Agreed," Ludmilla said. She extended her hand and shook Remo's formally, as if they were two diplomats who had spent months working out a meaningless, unworkable agreement of no interest to anyone but themselves.

"Okay. What do we do now?"

"We go to my hotel," Ludmilla said.

"And?"

"And we make beautiful, exquisite love. Seeing as how we are in love." Ludmilla smiled, the smile of awakening youth. It was one she did very well.

Remo nodded, as if making love were the most logical conclusion to an armistice that anyone could have devised. Together, arm in arm, they walked off—Remo looking forward, for the first time in years, to making love, and Ludmilla thinking of how she was going to find out the secret of his power so someone could kill this American maniac.

CHAPTER EIGHT

It was twenty-four hours since he'd left, but when Remo returned to his hotel room, Chiun was standing in the same position before the same set of yellow draperies, staring out at the same bright sun.

"It is all right," Chiun said without turning.

"What is all right?"

"It is all right that you are gone all night and you never let me know anything and I stay awake wondering all night if you are well or dead in an alley someplace. They have a Pig Alley in this city where people die all the time and how did I know

133

you weren't there? Especially since they named it after you?"

"I wasn't there."

Chiun turned and waved a long-nailed index finger in triumph. "Aha, but did I know that? Did you care enough to tell me?"

"No," said Remo honestly.

"Ingrate," said Chiun.

"True," said Remo. Nothing was going to spoil this day, the first day of the rest of his life, not even a bitching, carping, kvetching Chiun.

Remo smiled.

Chiun smiled.

"Ah, you are joking with me. You wanted to let me know you were well, but you couldn't? That's it, isn't it?"

"No," said Remo. "I haven't thought about you since yesterday morning. I didn't care whether you were worried or not. By the way, if you couldn't sleep, what's your sleeping mat doing out?"

"I tried to sleep, but I couldn't, I worried so much. I almost went out looking for you. You can see. The mat is barely wrinkled."

Remo said, "You could dance on it for eight hours and not wrinkle it." He said it mildly.

"But I didn't. I didn't even sleep on it."

"Chiun, I'm in love."

"Well, good,' said Chiun. "I forgive you then. It is a major step to take and I can understand why you were wandering the streets all night, thinking of the glories that are Sinanju and deciding to devote your life to our village, in a spirit of love. It is . . ."

"Chiun, I'm not in love with Sinanju. I'm in love with a woman."

Chiun looked shocked. He said nothing. Then he spat on the floor.

"All Frenchwomen are diseased," he said.

"She's not French."

"And American women are venial and stupid."

"She's not American."

Chiun tried a slight tentative smile. "A Korean girl? Remo, you are bringing home a . . ."

"A Russian," Remo said quickly.

"Aaaaagh," Chiun said. "Battalions of women with faces like gun butts and bodies like garages. A fine choice, meat-eater."

"She is a beauty," Remo said. "You shouldn't judge until you see. That's what you're always telling me."

"There are things you can judge without seeing, if you have any sense at all left in your head. You do not have to see every sunrise to know what the next one will look like. You do not have to spy on the moon every minute to make sure that it does not take the form of a square. Some things one knows. I know about Russian women."

"Not this one," Remo insisted.

"Where did you meet this creature?" Chiun asked.

"Woman, Chiun, not creature."

"Yes. Where did you met this meet this . . . one?"

"Woman, Chiun. I met her when she was trying to kill me."

"Very good," said Chiun. "And that of course told you it was love at first sight."

"Not really. For her, it had to grow."

"Good," Chiun said. "Now she is in love with you and will not try to kill you any more."

"Right."

Chiun shook his head. "Some day when all this world is ended and all the Masters of Sinanju who have ever lived gather with their ancestors to review the past, surely I will have the most elevated station of all. Because I have suffered the most. I have had to deal with you."

"Maybe not much longer," said Remo.

"I would meet this Russian barracks beauty with the face of a shovel and the form of a tractor."

"Good," said Remo. "I'd like you to meet her. I've told her a great deal about you."

"Will she try to kill me too?"

Remo shook his head. "I didn't tell her that much about you."

Remo and Chiun paused inside the door of the restaurant where they were to meet Ludmilla.

"There she is," Remo said. He pointed to the young Russian woman. No one in the restaurant saw him point because they were all already staring at Ludmilla, the men with lust, the women with envy.

"She is ugly," Chiun said.

"She has skin like cream," Remo said.

"Yes. That is one of the reasons she is ugly. The beautiful people have a different color skin."

"Look at her eyes."

"Yes, poor thing. Hers are straight. And violet. Violet eyes give very little protection against the sun. Marry that woman and you will have a blind crone on your hands before you get through your first thirty summers together."

"Have you ever seen hands like that?" Remo said. Ludmilla rose as she saw Remo. "A body like that?"

"No, thank the eternal powers that protect old men from shock. What an ugly creature."

"I love her," Remo said.

"I hate her," Chiun said. "I'm going home." He spun and brushed past Remo and walked back to their hotel, thinking deeply.

CHAPTER NINE

Walking to her hotel from the restaurant, Remo finally broke down. He had held strong through the salad, the soup, the main course, the coffee, and the dessert—none of which he had eaten—but Ludmilla finally got to him, and he told her the secret of his power.

It was candles. He had to sleep with candles lit in the room. If the candles weren't there or if they burned out, his strength vanished.

"Why did you not lose your power last night?" Ludmilla asked.

"Because I didn't sleep," Remo said. To prove his point, he stopped at a store and bought three thick red candles, the size of large instant coffee jars.

That night, as Remo slept in her playground-sized bed, Ludmilla went into the drawing room of her suite, made a telephone call, then extinguished the candles and lay down beside Remo.

Remo slept through her getting up and slept through her extinguishing of the candles and slept through her phone call and her return to bed.

He woke only long enough to take care of the man who sneaked into the room, wrapped powerful fingers around Remo's throat and began to squeeze. Remo impaled him on the bed post.

"You lied to me," Ludmilla screamed.

"Tell me about it in the morning."

"You said candles were the secret of your strength," she bawled. "You lied."

Remo shrugged and rolled over.

"I want you out of here. Now. And take your body with you."

"It's hard for me to go anywhere without it," Remo said.

"I don't mean *your* body, I mean that body on the end of my bed."

"Oh, no," Remo said, rolling over to look at Ludmilla. "Call the Russian embassy. They sent him; let them get him. I don't clean up any more bodies. That's all. Forget it. I won't."

Ludmilla reached out a long index finger and trailed it gently down Remo's chest from his throat to his navel. She smiled at him.

After Remo had disposed of the body under a pile of trash behind the hotel, he went back to Ludmilla's bed.

He did not sleep.

"Smitty, I need some cash." Remo drummed his fingers on the coffee table in the living room of his own hotel suite while the transatlantic phone call clicked and sputtered.

It took him a few seconds to realize the clicking and sputtering wasn't the phone system. It was Smith.

"Cash?" Smith was saying. "I just got a bill of yours for a thousand dollars."

"So? Is that so much?"

"From a shoe store?" Smith asked.

"Come on, Smitty, you know how it is when you find a pair of shoes you like. You buy a couple of pairs."

"One thousand dollars?"

"Well, I bought twenty-two pairs. It was important that my feet be clad just so."

"I see," Smith said drily. "And you have these twenty-two pairs of shoes with you, I presume."

"Of course not. Could I travel overseas with twenty-two pairs of shoes?"

"What'd you do with them?"

Remo sighed. "I gave them away. Smitty, don't you ever do anything but bicker, bicker, bicker about money? Here I've just saved the free world from disaster and you're complaining about my buying a measly couple of shoes. I need some cash."

"How much?"

"Fifty thousand dollars."

"You can't have it. That's too much for shoes."

"I'm not buying any more shoes. I need it for something else. Something real important."

"What?"

"I'm not telling."

"You can't have it."

"Okay. I'll raise it. I'll hire myself out to the highest bidder."

From the corner of the room, Chiun squeaked, "I bid twenty cents." Remo fixed him with an evil stare.

"All right," Smith said after a pause. "It'll be at the American Express office. Your passport in the name of Lindsay?"

"Wait a minute. Let me look." Remo looked through the top drawer of the chest and found the passport under a thing in waxed paper that seemed suspiciously like a dead fish.

"Yeah. Remo Lindsay."

"The money will be there in an hour."

"Good going, Smitty. You'll never regret this."

"Fine. What are you going to buy with it?"

"I can't tell you. But we'll name our first child after you."

"Oh?" said Smith, with more than his usual show of interest.

"Yes. Skinflint Tightwad Williams. That's if it's a boy."

"Goodbye, Remo."

Remo hung up and saw Chiun staring at him.

"It is about time that you and I had a talk," Chiun said.

"About what?"

"It is customary for a father to tell his son of certain things when the son is old enough to under-

141

stand them. In your case, I'll do it now rather than wait another ten years."

"You mean sex and like that?" asked Remo.

"Partially. And about women, good and bad."

"I don't want to hear about it."

Chiun bridged his fingers before him as if he had not heard Remo. "Now if you were able to select any woman in the world to be with, who would you choose?"

"Ludmilla," said Remo.

Chiun shook his head. "Be serious. I mean any woman in the world, not just a woman who is so desperate that she is willing to be seen with you. Let your imagination run amok. Any woman. Name her."

"Ludmilla."

"Remo. There are beautiful women in the world, even some with straight eyes. There are intelligent women and loving women. There are even some quiet women. Why would you pick this Russian tank-truck driver?"

"Because."

"Because why?"

Remo hesitated for only a split second. "Because I love her," he said.

Chiun lifted his eyes upward as if requesting God to pay close attention to the problems Chiun had to deal with in this life.

"Does she love you?"

"I think so," said Remo.

"Has she stopped trying to kill you yet?"

"Pretty soon now."

"Pretty soon now," Chiun mimicked. His voice

grew sincere and concerned. "Remo. Do you know who really loves you?"

"No. Who?" asked Remo, wondering if Chiun were going to let down his defenses. For once.

"Smith," said Chiun, after a pause.

"Bullshit," said Remo.

"The president of the United States. The automaker."

"Horse dung," said Remo. "He doesn't even know my name. He calls me 'those two.'"

Chiun yelled, "The people of Sinanju."

"Hogwash," Remo yelled back. "They don't even know I'm alive. If they can tolerate me, it's because I have something to do with those lazy slugs getting their gold shipment every November."

Chiun paused. He looked ceilingward as if gathering the courage to give Remo the name of one more person who really loved him. He looked back. "There is no point in discussing something with someone who can talk only in barnyard terms."

"Okay. Does that mean our discussion of the birds and the bees is over?"

"We did not once mention birds and bees, just other barnyard animals," Chiun said.

Remo rose. "I've got something to do."

"What is that?"

"I've got to buy a present."

"It is not my birthday," Chiun said.

"It is not for you," Remo said, walking to the door.

"See if I care," Chiun called. "See if the one who really . . ."

Remo paused. "Yes?"

"Never mind," Chiun said. "Go."

After picking up a bank draft for fifty thousand dollars at the American Express office, Remo went to a small jewelry shop on the Rue de la Paix.

The asking price for the diamond ring was forty thousand dollars, but by shrewd maneuvering, hard bargaining, and his incredible knowledge of the French language in which the negotiations were carried out, Remo managed to get the price up to fifty thousand. He pushed the bank draft over the counter to the French proprietor who had eyes that looked as if two hard-boiled eggs, had perforated his face, and a mustache that seemed to have been drawn on with one stroke of a woman's eyebrow pencil. The jeweler put the draft into the cash register quickly.

"Do you want it gift wrapped?" he said, in the first English he had spoken since Remo entered the shop.

"No. I'll eat it here. Of course I want it gift wrapped."

"There is a two-dollar charge for gift wrapping."

"Throw it in for free," Remo suggested.

"I would like to, but . . ." The man shrugged a Gallic shrug. "You know how it is."

"You know how this is too," said Remo. He punched the no-sale button on the register and plucked out the fifty-thousand-dollar bank draft. "Goodbye."

"Wait, sir. In your case we make an exception."

"I thought you might. Wrap it," Remo said.

When he presented the eight-carat stone to Ludmilla, she tore the paper, opened the box, looked at the ring, and threw it across the room.

144

"I already have diamonds," she said. "Do you think I would take a gift from a man who lies to me?"

"Okay, now I'll tell you the truth. I love you. I want you to come to America to live with me."

Ludmilla hissed at him. "Soooo, you think I give up my homeland that easily. Never. I am a Russian."

"Do you love me?"

"Maybe."

"Then come to America with me."

"No," Ludmilla said.

"My secret is in America," Remo said.

"Yes?" Ludmilla said.

"There is a spring there, a special water that makes any man invincible."

She came to his arms, and, without trying, he found himself flushing with warmth.

"Oh, Remo. I am glad you have at last told me the truth. Where is it, this spring?"

"In Las Vegas. That is a city," Remo said.

"I have never heard of it," Ludmilla said.

"It has much water," Remo said.

"And when do you want to go there?" she said.

"Tomorrow."

"Tonight," she said.

Remo kissed her lips. "Tomorrow," he said. "I have plans for tonight."

She looked at him with velvet eyes. "All right, tomorrow."

After Remo left, Ludmilla recovered the diamond ring from the floor. From a mother-of-pearl jewelry box in her top dresser drawer, she took a jeweler's loupe. She held the lens up to her eye and examined the ring carefully.

Only a VVF, she thought, a Very Very Fine. She noted a small carbon dot in the back of the stone. Worth no more than thirty thousand retail. But the American had probably paid forty thousand for it. Americans were such fools.

She put the ring in her jewelry box and then went to the phone to make a long distance call.

CHAPTER TEN

He was not going to the building at Dzerzhinsky Square. This time he was going to the Kremlin itself, and Marshal Denia decided not to wear his ribbons. He decided he was right when he saw the four men facing him. They wore dress uniforms with rows of ribbons on their chests. Each of them owned more ribbons than Denia had, and if he had worn his, it would have been a small admission that he was somehow less than them. By wearing none, he admitted only that he was different from them.

He looked at the clumps of ribbons on the four chests, each looking like an ear of Indian corn worn over the heart. Military decorations, he

147

thought, were a tribute not to bravery or competence but to longevity. The best and bravest soldiers he had ever seen had often not lived long enough to earn even one ribbon. In their youthful pride, they would have laughed at these four cadavers who stared now at Denia and demanded explanations of his "curious performance."

"Curious, comrade?" Denia asked the chairman of the board of inquiry. "The Treska has demolished America's most secret and powerful spy organization in Western Europe. In the process, true, we have lost some men. But we are continuously training new men to replace them. In months ... weeks, we will be back at full strength, while the Americans will never again put such a force in the field."

He said it and did not believe a word of it. Neither apparently did the chairman, a wizened old man with a face like cracked desert mud.

"And what guarantee do we have," the old man said, "that our new force will not be obliterated just as our last force was? What have you done about this?"

"I have isolated the special American agent who worked such damage on our men. I have infiltrated the entire apparatus. Soon we will have the answer to this riddle."

"Soon is not good enough."

"Soon is as good as it can be," Denia said, trying unsuccessfully to keep the edge from his voice. He looked to the other men sitting behind the stark wooden table in the small basement room. "In operations like ours, one occasionally encounters the unusual. You must study it before you can destroy it." One of the men on the panel had been a leader in Russia's scorched-earth policy when the Nazis invaded during World War II. Denia spoke in his direction. "It must be like the first foot soldiers ever to encounter a tank in battle. It would have been easy to run away. Or to panic and throw stones at the tank. But it was wise to watch and learn the monster's weaknesses. As our glorious people did against the Hitler hordes."

The old resistance leader nodded. Denia thought he had convinced one, before he realized, with disgust, that the old man was nodding himself to sleep. The man at the far right of the table had the look of a retired ribbon clerk and the manner of a lifelong cuckold. The look and manner disguised the fact that he was the premier's closest military advisor, a man whose bark could send even the secret police jumping. He had peopled one entire prison camp with his personal enemies.

"Your analogy is interesting, Gregory, but insufficient. We do not need descriptions of tactics that were successful thirty years ago in different situations. We need an up-to-the-minute report on what you are doing to eliminate this existing problem."

"One of our agents is with the American right now. She . . ."

"She?" Denia was interrupted by the aged chairman.

"Yes. Ludmilla Tchernova." Denia look at the man on the far right and smiled slightly. The man had been sleeping with Ludmilla for two years.

"Some of you know her," Denia said. "Ludmilla is one of our best agents. She is now on her way to America with this man. He thinks she has defected with him in the service of love. Her assignment is to find out what unusual weapons or techniques or powers this man uses, and then to report back to us so we can destroy him."

"When do you expect this will be accomplished?" asked the confidante of the premier.

Denia shrugged. "It is hard to say." From their faces, he could see that this did not go down well. "Within a week."

The premier's aide nodded. He looked at the other men at the table, then said, "All right. A week. And if that does not produce results, we shall have to try other measures."

Denia nodded in a military fashion. He tried not to show that he understood that those "other measures" would specifically exclude him, and that one week and a sexy Russian courtesan were all that stood between him and exile.

Or worse.

On the Air France plane to New York, Remo sat between Ludmilla and Chiun, who kept asking the stewardesses to bring him more magazines. He would scan each magazine quickly, then lean across Remo to point out to the young Russian woman stories about the latest atrocities behind the Iron Curtain.

Ludmilla kept her face fixed grimly on the window.

"All right, Chiun, knock it off," Remo said.

"I am just being friendly," Chiun said. He flipped the pages of the magazine in his lap, then excitedly pushed it across Remo into Ludmilla's hands. "See. The advertisement for a new tractor.

You will love America. They have many tractors for you to drive."

Ludmilla snatched the magazine from Chiun and slammed it to the floor then threw her arms up over her head in desperation. The diamond ring on the index finger of her right hand glistened an eight-carat glisten.

"How much of this abuse must I tolerate?" she said.

"Abuse?" Chiun said. "Abuse? What abuse? Now a friendly gesture and warm conversation is abuse?" He talked to Remo as if Ludmilla was not there. "Really, Remo, I cannot see what you like about this one."

Remo growled. Ludmilla turned her face stonily toward the window. Chiun looked back at another news magazine. He recognized a picture and pushed the magazine into Remo's lap.

"Look, Remo. The woman. Isn't she beautiful?"

"Yeah," Remo said without spirit. "Beautiful."

"I knew you would like her," Chiun said. He sat back in his seat and stared at the magazine. The woman was the kind Remo liked. Long in the leg and big in the chest. The man was hopeless. If a racehorse could fit into a dress, Remo would fall in love with it.

Chiun read the caption under the picture of the half-clad Hollywood star who was making her nightclub debut with a new act that featured partial nudity and total witlessness.

"Remo. Where did you say we were going?" Chiun asked.

"Ludmilla and I are going to Las Vegas. I don't know where you're going."

151

Chiun nodded and said softly, "I might just go to Las Vegas too." He read the caption again. The Hollywood star was opening her new night club act at the Crystal Hotel in Las Vegas. Chiun nodded. There was only one thing to do: fight ugly with ugly.

How simple it all would have been though if Remo had been taken with one of the lovely maidens of Sinanju. How simple.

Chiun mused as Remo got up and went to the men's room in the front of the first-class section.

Ludmilla waited until he disappeared into the small room, then moved over into his seat. She looked at Chiun.

Eyes like a cow, he thought.

"Why do you hate me?" she said.

"I do not hate you. I do not understand what he"—Chiun nodded toward the bathroom—"sees in you."

"Perhaps love."

"He has all the love he needs."

"From whom?"

"From me," Chiun said.

"You are jealous of me, aren't you?"

"Jealous? The Master jealous? Do you think I care what that pale piece of pig's ear does? No? Except for this. I have invested years of my life in this one, and I cannot sit by and watch him turn into mud in the hands of one whose only wish is to kill him."

"You think that's all I want?" she said.

"I know that is all you want. It is written on your face in foot-high letters. Only a fool could fail to see it."

"A fool. Or a man in love." Ludmilla laughed. She was still laughing when Remo returned to his seat.

"I'm glad to see you two are hitting it off better," Remo said.

Ludmilla laughed again. Chiun grunted and turned away, across the aisle, to look out the windows on the other side of the plane.

Two important meetings were held later that day.

In Washington, the Secretary of State stood before the President's desk, waiting for the Commander in Chief to finish stapling together a small pile of papers. The President carefully positioned the stapler at the upper-left-hand corner of the sheets. He held it accurately in place with the thumb and middle finger of his left hand. He raised his right fist up in front of his forehead and slammed it downward at the stapler.

And missed.

His right fist slammed into his unprepared left hand. The stapler slid away. Papers bounced into the air. The President jerked his left hand to his mouth and began sucking on the injured fingers.

He sighed, looked up, and remembered the Secretary of State. Odd that the man should be standing in the center of the room. Why hadn't he come closer to the desk?

He beckoned the Secretary to come nearer. With a cautionary look at the stapler, the Secretary waddled slowly forward.

"What is it?" the President asked.

"I have just returned from a closed-door meeting

of the Senate Foreign Affairs Committee," the man said. His voice was a slow professional chant that sounded as if he were going to begin a disquisition on mathematical theory in the Golden Age of Greece.

"Yeah?" mumbled the President around the fingers that were still stuck in his mouth. The hurt was starting to leave them now. If he was lucky, he wouldn't get blood blisters under the nails.

"They had heard that somehow we have scored a major intelligence victory in Europe—and of course they wish to investigate this."

"Ummmmmm," the President sucked.

"I told them that I had no knowledge of such a victory and certainly we did not have anything to do with securing it, if victory it was."

"Ummmmmm," the President said.

"They did not believe me. They think this administration has defied their Congressional prerogatives and gone off on some kind of intelligence adventure."

"Ummmmm."

"They will call me and the CIA Director to testify, probably in the next few days."

"Ummmmm. Seems logical."

"So don't you think, Mr. President, that it is now time to tell me just what has occurred in Europe?"

The President took his fingers from his mouth. "No," he said. "What you know is accurate. The United States took no action with any of its agencies to bring about whatever Congress thinks may have happened in Europe. Stick with that. It's true."

The Secretary of State looked unhappy, but he nodded.

"Tell me," the President said. "Do you think the Congress really wants the Russians to beat us?"

"No, Mr. President," the Secretary said. "But they are pandering to those who do."

"Who are?"

"The press. The young. The radicals. Everyone who hates America because they have been rewarded, by life here, in a manner that far exceeds their worth."

The President nodded. He liked it when the Secretary was philosophical. The Secretary waited, then turned again to the door.

His hand was on the knob when the President spoke.

"Mr. Secretary," he said.

"Yes sir?"

"I've just about had it with these people. I want you to know. If Congress puts any heat on you over this European business . . ."

"Yes?"

"I'm going to hang them up by their balls."

When the Secretary of State met his eyes, the President of the United States winked.

The other important meeting was held later that day, backstage at the Crystal Hotel in Las Vegas where Miss Jacquanne Juice—she was always billed as "Miss Jacquanne Juice," although there had not been, since she was eleven years old, any danger of anyone's mistaking her for Mr. Jacquanne Juice—was trying to explain to a costume designer what was wrong with the bra she was wearing.

"Look, I'm going to flash my galonkers at them

for the finale. But it would help if I could get them out of the bra. The goddamn thing doesn't open up."

The designer was a small man with long white-blond hair. His wrists were thinner than the woman's. His fingers were inoffensive as he touched the front clip on the bra the young woman wore and showed her how a simple squeeze on both sides of the strap would pop it open.

"See?" he said, as the bra exploded open and Miss Jacquanne Juice was left standing bare-breasted in the middle of the rehearsal stage. Around them, throats cleared and movement ceased. Men who a second before had been busy doing things, professional things on which their livelihoods depended, stopped, no longer caring about anything except Miss Jacquanne Juice's mammary glands.

"It's easy," the costume designer said.

"It's frigging impossible," the woman answered. "It's easy for you, you're fooling around with some-body else's tits all day. For me, it's hard. I keep clawing at this thing and clawing at it. If I ever get the thing open, I'll be standing there, my jugs cov-ered with blood. Is that what you want for a fi-nale? Is it? A frigging horror show? You going to bring bats down out of the balcony? Hah? Oh, crap. Doesn't anyone around here care about me? Am I always going to be just a piece of meat?"

She looked around the stage and found that ev-ery pair of male eyes within sighting distance was fixed upon her breasts. Some of them were nod-ding answers to her question. '

Except one.

A small, aged Oriental wearing a white robe looked at her with hazel eyes that were wise beyond wisdom, and he smiled at her slightly and nodded, a nod of sympathy and understanding. The small movement of his head seemed to send waves across the room to where Miss Jacquanne Juice stood, waves that enveloped her with knowledge of her own womanhood and personhood. She suddenly felt bare-breasted, and she pulled the bra's cups closed around her front and fumbled with the clip.

"We'll work on it later," she told the clothing designer, then brushed past him to speak with the old Oriental.

She stood in front of the old man, staring down at the white brocade robe, and then, because she could think of nothing to say but had to say something, she said: "Did you know I have an IQ of 138?"

"I can see that," Chiun said. He had never heard anyone describe her bust size with the letters IQ before, but if she claimed to be a 138, he believed it, because she was cowlike like most American women were or aspired to be.

"And yet," he added, "they treat you badly. They all want something from you, but in turn they give nothing."

He patted a spot next to him on the top of the wardrobe trunk, indicating that she should sit down.

"How did you know that?" she said.

"They all want and take but never give. There is none you can trust, none who cares about you as much as he cares about himself."

Miss Jacquanne Juice nodded.

"But how did you know? You're some kind of a guru, aren't you? How did you know?"

"It is ever thus with leaders. With stars as well as with emperors. The most difficult thing is to find one you can trust, someone without motives of his own, someone who cares for you as you and does not wish something from you."

"Oh. All my life. Looking and looking," Miss Jacquanne Juice said. She put her head on Chiun's shoulder. He patted her bare back gently, to console her for a world so cruel that it paid her only a quarter-million dollars for two weeks of breast-baring in the middle of the Nevada desert.

"You can stop searching," Chiun said. "There *is* one who cares about you." He turned his face to look into her eyes.

"I believe. I believe," she said. She pushed her face closer to his shoulder. "Oh, what a feeling to know there is someone who cares."

Chiun patted her back again, this time searching out a precise spot for tapping with his long finger-nails.

"And you must let me . . ." She sighed as she felt the currents from Chiun's fingers pass through her body. "You must let me do something for you."

She looked up at Chiun hopefully. He shook his head. "There is nothing I need, my child."

"There must be something, something I can do for you."

"Nothing," Chiun said.

"Something. Anything. A gesture."

Chiun paused, long enough to appear thoughtful. Then he said:

"Well, there is just one little thing."

That afternoon, after a platoon of hotel personnel had made her comfortable in her room, Ludmilla pressed Remo for the exact location of the secret spring that gave him his powers.

Remo sighed. "Look, we're in America. You promised to give this a try, and maybe to stay. Now can't you stop being a government honcho for a while?"

"This has nothing to do with government. This has to do with honor. And trust. And love. You promised me and you should live up to your promise."

"It's not far from here," Remo said. "Ten, twenty miles."

"When will we go there?"

"Now if you want."

"Tomorrow. Tomorrow will be better. And we will have a picnic. And we will make love out in the sand."

Remo, who knew more about sand and desert heat than Ludmilla, nodded, but the more he nodded, the more appealing the idea sounded.

"And now you must leave," Ludmilla said.

"Why?"

"Because I need my rest. Go. Go. I will see you later and be beautiful for you."

Remo nodded again and left, and walked whistling down the hallway toward the steps to his own room. He did not hear the silent movements behind him as Chiun came from behind a potted palm and walked to Ludmilla's door.

Inside the telephone rang. Ludmilla said "hello"

and waited while the operator opened the line on her call to Moscow. Chiun could only hear her half of the conversation with Marshal Denia.

"Yes. Probably tomorrow we will go there. Oh, good. You are coming? When will you get here? Wonderful. I long to see you again. I will not go there until you arrive."

Chiun rapped on the door, and heard the telephone quickly hung up. When Ludmilla opened the door, her face was first surprised, then annoyed.

"Oh. You."

"Yes. I hope I did not disturb anything important." He smiled at her and Ludmilla knew that Chiun had heard the call. What she did not know was that Chiun, at that moment, was only a hair away from killing her to protect Remo. But he did not strike, because Remo would never have believed in the necessity of the act.

"Nothing important," she said. "What do you want?"

"I am inviting you and Remo to dinner tonight. As my guests."

"Oh, well . . ."

"You must," Chiun said. "You and I must be friends."

She paused, then acceded. "If you insist."

"I do. I insist. Remo will call for you. I will see to it."

Ludmilla laughed. "I have already seen to it, old man. He will call for me whenever I wish."

"As you would have it," Chiun said and walked away, angered because the woman was right. Remo was her slave.

CHAPTER ELEVEN

"I don't know why you keep that old man hanging around anyway," Ludmilla said.

"I've grown accustomed to his face," Remo said, and sipped his mineral water to turn off the conversation.

They sat at a front table in the Crystal Hotel supper club. Chiun had insisted that all the arrangements be left to him, and when Remo and Ludmilla arrived, the headwaiter smiled at them, showed them to a front row table, was polite, and set the indoor record for Las Vegas—a mark that would live forever, Remo decided—by refusing a tip.

161

Ludmilla persisted. "It would be different if that old goblin gave something to you. But nothing except complaints. This is how you spend your life? Listening to him complain? Why is he here? Why is he with us?"

"He's really a nice old geezer," Remo said. "Besides, he has his strong points."

"Yes?"

"Yes," said Remo.

"Tell me one of his strong points."

Remo thought a moment. How to tell her that Chiun was more deadly than a whole military division, more powerful than plutonium, more accurate than calculus. How to tell her?

"He's all right," Remo said. "He knows a lot of things."

"He knows how to get old and sponge off his betters and his youngers," Ludmilla said. "Too bad for you that you do not send him away."

"Well . . ." Remo was noncommittal. "That's the way it goes."

He was spared further conversation by the crowd. Instead of a roar, there was a hush and then every voice in the room was silent, and Remo turned toward the entrance to the supper club.

Walking down the aisle through the tables was Chiun, wearing a black robe, and on his arm, towering a head over him, was Miss Jacquanne Juice, headliner of the show at the Crystal Hotel. She wore a scanty white gown and nothing else.

Remo looked at them, as did every other pair of eyes in the room.

"Stop looking at her," Ludmilla said.

"I'm not," Remo said. "I'm looking at Chiun. The old fox is enjoying this."

There was a spattering of applause. Like a heavyweight fighter, Chiun waved, a king's gesture to quiet the unruly mob.

Then Chiun and Jacquanne were at the table and the headwaiter helped seat them, and slowly the room returned to its steady buzzing as customers went back to their drinks.

Chiun smiled. "Remo, this is Miss Jacquanne Juice. Or something like that. This is Remo, who is better than he looks."

Chiun stopped and Remo cleared his throat.

"Oh," Chiun said. "This . . ." He waved toward Ludmilla. "This is a Russian woman. This is Miss Jacquanne Juice."

Ludmilla nodded. Jacquanne looked at her, then said, "You're beautiful."

Chiun nudged her under the table, but Remo said, "Yes, isn't she?"

"So are you," Chiun said to Jacquanne. "You are most beautiful. The most beautiful woman Remo has ever seen. Isn't that right, Remo?"

Remo shrugged and looked at Ludmilla.

"Isn't that right, Remo?" Chiun persisted.

"What is your name?" Jacquanne asked Ludmilla.

"Ludmilla."

"You are beautiful. Truly beautiful."

"Thank you." It did not occur to Ludmilla to return the compliment; it did not occur to Jacquanne to hint at it.

Chiun said, "You are truly beautiful" to Jacquanne. "Don't you think so, Remo?"

Remo nodded, reluctantly.

"And she makes a very good living, Remo. She has her own band, and people who walk around fastening her brassieres and everything," Chiun explained.

Remo nodded again.

Ludmilla said, "Remo, I have a headache. I think I'd like to go back to my room."

"All right." Remo stood.

"You are coming back, though, Remo, right?" said Chiun.

"I doubt it." Ludmilla answered for Remo.

Chiun looked dejected. Jacquanne could not take her eyes off the Russian woman. Remo shrugged.

"Good night, Chiun. Good night, Miss . . ." Remo said.

"Juice," said Chiun. "Jacquanne Juice."

"Good night, Miss Juice," Remo said.

"Good night," said Ludmilla. "Miss Juice. Old man." And when Chiun met her eyes, she winked—the wink of a winner to a loser, and then she turned and led Remo from the supper club.

They had gone only two steps toward the exit when Remo was stopped by an order, barked by Chiun in Korean.

Remo turned. He felt Ludmilla stop and look back also. Chiun, speaking a fast flow of Korean words, picked up the dinner knife at the table. He held it in his left hand, handle between his fingertips, then with the tip of his right index finger struck the knife three times, with no more apparent force than if he were poking someone in the chest to make a point. The first two pokes broke off pieces of the steel knifeblade; the third

164

poke split the silver alloy handle into two pieces which fell on the table in front of Chiun.

He nodded to Remo who nodded back before pulling Ludmilla toward the door. She was looking over the shoulder at Chiun and the pieces of knife in front of him.

"What did he say?" she asked.

"It was Korean," Remo said. " 'Even a knife may shatter; even a strong man may fall.' "

Ludmilla was still looking over her shoulder, her eyes narrowed.

"How did he do that with the knife?"

"Who knows?" said Remo.

"Can you do it?"

"I don't know. Maybe. Chiun understands more about objects than I do. It has something to do with vibrations."

They were at the door and Remo led the way out. Ludmilla kept staring at Chiun until the door closed behind them.

The next day Marshal Denia arrived in Las Vegas.

CHAPTER TWELVE

Ludmilla had begged off the trip to the desert to see Remo's magic spring, pleading an upset stomach; Remo had gone out to walk around Las Vegas; and Chiun was alone in their room when a messenger came.

"I must see you. L."

Chiun crumpled the message and dropped it on the floor, then walked up to Ludmilla's room.

When he entered, she was seated at her dressing table, her back to Chiun, wearing only a bluish robe that made her skin seem to glow a pale yellow. She smiled at Chiun in the mirror, a dropped-eyes coy smile, then carefully closed her open robe before she spun on her chair and faced him.

"I have asked you to come so I could apologize to you," she said. "I have treated you badly."

"I am always treated badly," Chiun said.

"I know how it must be. No one understands you; they ask much of you but give nothing in return."

Chiun nodded. The faint tendrils of hair over his ears continued nodding after his head had stopped.

"Well, I do not wish to be one of those ungrateful ones," said Ludmilla. She rose and walked to Chiun who stood just inside the door. She took his two hands in hers. "I am sorry," she said.

"Why?" said Chiun.

"I am sorry for my rudeness, but more for my stupidity. I realize all I could learn from your wisdom and your gentleness and like a fool I have rejected that gift of friendship you offered me."

Chiun nodded again.

She reached her right hand to touch the side of his face. As her left arm left her side, the front of her dressing gown slipped open. She moved even closer to Chiun, so close their bodies almost touched. "Can you forgive me?" she said.

"Yes," said Chiun. He looked down at Ludmilla's flawless skin, shadowed yellow by the blue of the gown. "You are a lovely woman," he said.

She smiled at him again and left her hand on the side of his face. "Thank you," she said. "But beauty is a gift of God; wisdom is an achievement of character."

"That is true," Chiun said. "That is true. Most never see that truth."

"Most never have their eyes fully open," she said. She leaned even closer to him.

"And what of Remo?" Chiun said.

Ludmilla shrugged. The movement almost, but not quite, released her breasts from her gown. "Who looks at the sapling when he stands on the edge of the forest?"

And again Chiun nodded, and as he did, Ludmilla leaned forward and moved her face down to his, searching for his lips with hers. As she found them, she said softly, "I have never been made love to by a Master of Sinanju."

And afterwards, she said—and meant it—"Never before like that."

She lay next to Chiun in her bed, his body still clothed in his red kimono, hers covered by a sheet, and laughed.

"To think of Remo telling me his power came from a magic spring."

"The child likes to joke," Chiun said.

"But the power is Sinanju, isn't it?" she said.

"No, beauteous one. The power is within each person; Sinanju is the key that unlocks the power."

"And you are the Master." She said it in a tone of reverential awe, as if she could not believe that Chiun was with her.

Then she rolled on her side toward him, put her left hand on his face, and said, "Show me a trick. Do something for me."

"Sinanju is not meant for tricks," he said.

"But for me? Just once. Just let me see some of your awesome power. Please?"

"Only for you," Chiun said.

"Remo told me it was vibrations," she said.

"Sometimes it is vibrations," Chiun said. "It is in knowing what you deal with that you make each thing a weapon. Each thing has its own vibrations, is its own central being, and to use it, you must first understand it, then become it."

As he spoke, Chiun used a fingernail to bust open the pillow under his head. He sat up and pulled out two small feathers, each an inch-long piece of fluffy down.

"What could be softer than the feather?" he said. "Yet, it is soft only because we use it for softness. We need not."

Hands moving faster than eye could follow, Chiun raised the two feathers, one in each hand, to his eyes, and then splashed his hands forward toward the opposite wall of the room.

The two small feathers left his fingertips like supersonic darts, hit the wooden wall with simultaneous "pings," and buried themselves into the wood panel where they stayed, vibrating, in the breeze of the overhead air conditioner, like miniature plumes.

"Marvelous," Ludmilla said. "Can I do that? Can I learn?"

"Only after much practice. Much time," said Chiun.

"I have much time," she said, pulling him back onto the pillow next to her. "And I want to learn everything you can teach me."

"And I will teach you," Chiun said. "Things you never even dreamed of before."

Later, Ludmilla had a wonderful idea. Her upset stomach had vanished, so why didn't she and Chiun drive out into the desert and look for a spring, then tell Remo they had found his magic spring. It would be a joke. A wonderful joke, she thought. And if Chiun wanted to change, he could; she would arrange for a car and driver, and meet him in front of the hotel in fifteen minutes.

Chiun looked at her and she could see in his eyes that he wanted to do this thing very much, so without even waiting for an answer, she patted his face again and walked with him to the door.

He stopped in the doorway and looked up at her violet eyes.

"You are a most beautiful woman," he said.

Ludmilla blushed and then closed the door behind him. She had things to do and she didn't need Chiun around. No fool like an old fool, she thought, as she went to the telephone.

Twenty minutes later, she and Chiun were sitting in the back of a Rolls Royce on its way out of Las Vegas on Boulder Highway. Chiun wore a thin black robe.

In the front seat was their driver, a pudgy mustached man, and two other men who, Ludmilla explained, were guides to the desert around Las Vegas. Each had a neck as big as the average man's thigh. They wore hats and stared straight ahead. Ludmilla's eyes looked up and caught the eyes of the driver in the rear-view mirror.

Field Marshal Gregory Denia smiled at her. The courtesan had done her work well. First, they would finish this old man, and then even the score with the American, Remo. The courtesan had done very well.

Remo lost $2,350 playing roulette but won $4.00 in nickels playing slot machines before getting back to the hotel, where the first thing he saw was the crumpled note Chiun had dropped on the floor.

I must see you. L.

He would talk to Chiun about that. Intercepting a note obviously meant for Remo, and then just throwing it away. He steamed on his way up the stairs to Ludmilla's room.

There was no answer to his knock, but the door was open and inside, in an envelope, he found another note: this time for him.

Remo. I do not wish to see you again. The old one has shown me what true love is. I am heart and body the woman of the Master of Sinanju. Goodbye. Ludmilla.

Remo crumpled the note and dropped it. His brain whirling in confusion, he spun and looked at the room. The bed was unmade, and Remo could see that it had been used, but not for sleeping.

"Chink bastard. Dirty two-timing conniving slant-eyed Korean fink," Remo shouted. He slammed his fist into the wall, splintering the wood panel, and then, the blood rising up in his temples, he walked from the room with a mission in his mind. He was going to find and kill Chiun. Search and destroy.

171

It took him five minutes to learn that Chiun and Ludmilla had driven out into the desert in a rented Rolls Royce and only five seconds to steal a car to follow them.

Minutes later, Remo was racing across the desert highway, his foot holding the gas pedal down to the floor, the stolen Ford a projectile, moving at 120 miles an hour down the straight-as-string two-lane road.

And ten minutes later he saw the big Rolls Royce parked alongside the highway, and he saw footprints through the sand leading toward a small hill seventy-five yards from the road.

He turned off the key and skidded the car to a stop and was out, on the ground, before the car stopped rocking on its springs.

There were a lot of footprints leading through the sand but Remo was interested only in one pair—those of Chiun's sandals, which scuffed along in the middle of all the other footprints.

Remo took the hill in three giant strides. He was looking down into a natural depression, a bowl in the ground surrounded by an almost perfectly circular hill. Sitting in the sand, his black robe swirled about him, was Chiun. His arms were folded and he looked implacably ahead.

"Dink bastard," Remo shouted and ran down the hill into the natural amphitheater, before it occured to him to wonder where Ludmilla was.

"Rat bastard," Remo yelled again.

Chiun looked up. "I have waited for you."

"And so have we." The voice came from behind Remo. He turned and saw three men and

172

Ludmilla coming down the hill toward him. The three men carried pistols in their hands.

Remo looked from Ludmilla to Chiun, then back to the woman and the three men.

Two of the men stopped behind Remo and trained their weapons on him, while the third man, Marshal Denia, and Ludmilla walked past Remo and stopped in front of Chiun.

"Ludmilla," Remo called weakly. She did not respond. She did not even look at him. Denia did.

"This is a better catch than I hoped for. First the old man, and then you, American. The spilled blood of the Treska will be avenged."

"Go ahead," Remo said. "Kill the son of a bitch."

Denia cocked his revolver and pointed it at Chiun, who sat still only six feet away from him, his arms still folded.

"Chiun," Remo called. But Chiun did not answer, and Remo suddenly realized the truth. Chiun was going to let himself be killed.

"Chiun," he yelled again.

"Only one can save my life," Chiun said finally.

"I'll save it," Remo said. "I'll save it. Just for the pleasure of killing you myself, you two-timing fraud."

Chiun shut his eyes. "The House of Sinanju has lived on a frail thread for thousands of years," he said. "If it must be broken now by a Master I have chosen and I have trained, then these eyes will not see it. I welcome this Russian death."

As if to oblige, Denia raised his pistol at arm's length before him, taking aim at Chiun's forehead. Remo saw Ludmilla reach into her handbag and remove her cigarette case and begin to light a cigarette.

"I'll save it," Remo yelled. "I'm going to save it and then I'm going to wring your scrawny neck."

He lashed back with both feet, kicking up and out. He felt the backs of his shoes crack into two gun-bearing hands. His own hands hit the sand and Remo pulled his weight up and forward, then slammed back with the toes of his feet into two throats. He knew without turning that both men were dead, and he used their throats for a toehold to break across the sand toward Denia and Chiun and Ludmilla.

"Gregory," Ludmilla said when she saw Remo coming toward them. Denia turned and pointed his pistol at Remo who stopped, ten feet away, apparently neutralized by Denia's gun.

"So these are the tricks of Sinanju," Denia said with a smile. "In some other age, American, I would have liked to learn them." He sighed heavily. "But this is not the time or the place."

He squeezed the trigger and fired a shot at Remo. At ten feet, it missed. Remo had slipped off to the left, and now he was standing motionless in a new spot. Denia fired again, and missed again, and now Remo was moving slowly across the sand toward him, high on his toes, scurrying, slipping, and sliding, and Denia fired again and again and again and ... click! The revolver was empty, and Remo made one final move in, plucked the revolver from Denia's hand, and replaced it in the Russian spy's throat. It went in barrel first and Denia coughed, as if he had swallowed a piece of food down the wrong tube, and then he reached

174

for his throat but the gun butt got in his way. His hand closed on it, and it looked as if he had just punctured his own throat with his own gun, and then he exhaled, a single loud hiss of air, and fell heavily onto his side in the sand.

Chiun opened his eyes and saw Remo towering over him. Remo rocked back and forth on his feet as if building up enough inertial energy to strike.

"You're dead, Chiun," he said. "You made love to her. My woman. How could you?"

"It was easy," Chiun said mildly. "She asked me to. She would have asked anyone to, if she thought they could give her a way to kill you."

Remo blinked, then looked from Chiun to Ludmilla. She shook her head at him. "He lies," she said. "He lies. He came to my room and took me by force. It was awful. Terrible."

Remo looked back to Chiun who still sat motionless in the sand. "Ask yourself, Remo. What are these Russians doing here? Who were they sent to kill? Who led them to you and to me?"

"Enough of this, Remo," Ludmilla said. "Kill this old fool and let us be off. In Russia, you can have a new life with me."

Remo hesitated. His hands clenched and unclenched.

"Do it now, or I leave," Ludmilla said. "I will not stand here burning in the hot sun waiting for a fool to make a decision." She flicked her gold lighter and raised it to the cigarette at her lips.

Remo looked down at Chiun. His hands were folded in his lap; his eyes were closed, but his face was tilted upward, and his throat was a target as open as an Irish drunk's mouth. A toe shot would take him out for good. Rip out the throat and leave him in the sand.

"I'm waiting, Remo," Ludmilla said. Remo still hesitated, and Ludmilla walked past him to the body of Marshal Denia. "If you won't do it, I'll do it myself." She picked up the empty revolver and turned to aim it at Chiun.

His left arm flailed out around his body, and the side of his hand came up, hit into the end of Ludmilla's gold cigarette holder and slammed it back into her throat. She looked at Remo with large violet eyes, made larger by shock and surprise, then she smiled at him—the smile of sudden joy—but she still didn't have it right, and she died.

Remo dropped to his knees and buried his face on Ludmilla's body. He wept. Chiun rose to his feet and moved silently to Remo and patted him on the shoulder.

"She wanted only to kill you, my son."

With almost invisible pressure, his patting motion turned into a grasp that lifted Remo up from the sand and placed him on his feet.

"Come," Chiun said. Still holding Remo's shoulder, he walked him away toward the cars behind the small hill.

At the top of the hill, Remo looked down at the body of Ludmilla and his voice broke again.

"I loved her, Little Father."

"How long are you going to hold this against me?" Chiun asked. "Am I going to hear nothing but complaints for the rest of the afternoon?"

A week later, the Senate Foreign Affairs Committee, which had given the Secretary of State and the CIA Director a tough going-over behind closed doors, was called to the office of the President of the United States.

The President dumped out a manila envelope containing some two dozen passports. He looked around the room at the thirteen senators who sat in soft leather chairs facing his desk.

"Those are the passports of twenty-four American agents who have been killed since you clowns began meddling with our intelligence setup."

The chairman of the committee began to rise to protest. The President of the United States put a large sinewy hand on his shoulder and pushed him back into his chair.

"Sit still and shut up."

The President dumped out another envelope filled with passports.

"Those are the fake cover passports of the Russian spies who killed our men. They're dead now, too."

He looked slowly, around the room, meeting and holding every man's eyes in turn.

"Now you can make something of this if you want to. It's your right to do that. But let me tell you something. Mess with this and I'm going to hang all your asses on a garage door. When I'm done telling the American people how you were responsible for twenty-four murders, you'll be lucky not to be indicted yourself. For murder. You got it?"

No one spoke.

"Any questions?"

No one spoke.

Three days later, the Senate Foreign Affairs

Committee decided unanimously that there was no substance to the reports of major espionage activity in Western Europe by the United States and decided to drop its planned investigation.

THE PENETRATOR

by Lionel Derrick

Mark Hardin. Discharged from the army, after service in Vietnam. His military career was over. But *his* war was just beginning. His reason for living and reason for dying become the same—to stamp out crime and corruption wherever he finds it. He is deadly; he is unpredictable; and he is dedicated. He is The Penetrator!

Read all of him in:

Order		Title	Book No.	Price
_____	# 1	THE TARGET IS H	P236	$ .95
_____	# 2	BLOOD ON THE STRIP	P237	$ .95
_____	# 3	CAPITOL HELL	P318	$ .95
_____	# 4	HIJACKING MANHATTAN	P338	$ .95
_____	# 5	MARDI GRAS MASSACRE	P378	$ .95
_____	# 6	TOKYO PURPLE	P434	$1.25
_____	# 7	BAJA BANDIDOS	P502	$1.25
_____	# 8	THE NORTHWEST CONTRACT	P540	$1.25
_____	# 9	DODGE CITY BOMBERS	P627	$1.25
	#10	THE HELLBOMB FLIGHT	P690	$1.25

TO ORDER

Please check the space next to the book/s you want, send this order form together with your check or money order, include the price of the book/s and 25¢ for handling and mailing, to:

PINNACLE BOOKS, INC. / P.O. Box 4347
Grand Central Station / New York, N. Y. 10017

☐ Check here if you want a free catalog.

I have enclosed $_____ check_____ or money order_____ as payment in full. No C.O.D.'s.

Name_____

Address_____

City_____ State_____ Zip_____

(Please allow time for delivery)

THE "BUTCHER,"
the only man to leave
the Mafia—and live!
A man forever on the run,
unable to trust anyone,
condemned to a life
of constant violence!

THE BUTCHER SERIES

Order		Title	Book #	Price
_____	# 1	KILL QUICK OR DIE	P011	.95
_____	# 2	COME WATCH HIM DIE	P025	.95
_____	# 3	KEEPERS OF DEATH	P603	1.25
_____	# 4	BLOOD DEBT	P111	.95
_____	# 5	DEADLY DEAL	P152	.95
_____	# 6	KILL TIME	P197	.95
_____	# 7	DEATH RACE	P228	.95
_____	# 8	FIRE BOMB	P608	1.25
_____	# 9	SEALED WITH BLOOD	P279	.95
_____	#10	THE DEADLY DOCTOR	P291	.95
_____	#11	VALLEY OF DEATH	P332	.95
_____	#12	KILLER'S CARGO	P429	1.25
_____	#13	BLOOD VENGEANCE	P539	1.25
_____	#14	AFRICAN CONTRACT	P583	1.25
_____	#15	KILL GENTLY, BUT SURE	P671	1.25
_____	#16	SUICIDE IN SAN JUAN	P726	1.25
_____	#17	THE CUBANO CAPER	P794	1.25
_____	#18	THE U.N. AFFAIR	P843	1.25
_____	#19	MAYDAY OVER MANHATTAN	P869	1.25
_____	#20	THE HOLLYWOOD ASSASSIN	P893	1.25